Step-Mommy!
(The Book)
Feminization to BDSM to gender transformation!

includes the complete series:

The Feminizing Step-Mother!
My Step-Mommy Feminized Me!
Revenge of the Step-Mommy!
The Step-Mommy and the Lady Boy!

Grace Mansfield

I Changed My Husband into a Woman!

Check it out at…

https://gropperpress.wordpress.com

TABLE OF CONTENTS

NOVELS BY GRACE MANSFIELD AND ALYCE THORNDYKE

My Husbands Funny Breasts
Too Tough to Feminize
I Changed My Husband into a Woman
The Emasculation Project
The Feminization Games
A Woman Unleashed
The Stepforth Husband
Revenge of the Stepforth Husbands
The Sissy Ride
Feminized by a Ghost
The Curse of the Werefem
Silithia
The Big Tease
Womanland
The Man Who Abused a Woman
A Woman Gone Mad
Sissy Slaves the Book
The Once and Future Man
The Day the Democrats Turned the Republicans
The Broken Man
Breaking Jack
Monastery of Broken Men
Ship of Broken Men
The Horny Wizard of Oz
The Lusty Land of Oz
Hucows, Bully Boys and Were-Cows
the Sissy Transition
I was Feminized and Dominated!
Toy for a Sex Monster!
Femwood Mansion!
Female Different!
Sex Crazy!
The Long, Hot Feminization!
Fade to Pink!

You can find bundles and collections at

https://gropperpress.wordpress.com

A Note from the Author!

Step Mommies are fun!

They usually marry older men, and then they have to unleash their sexual attentions on younger men, like…step-sons!

Shiela is a real babe! She's a MILF! And she is hu-u-ungry!

Then there's Lucas, a poor, sweet, innocent lad who comes home for the summer. He has no idea what is awaiting him, and what Shiela is about to do.

Shiela, you see, lives to consume young lovers.

Go Step-Mommy!

STAY HORNY!
Gracie

She dominated, she chastised, she was…

The Feminizing Step-Mother!

Grace Mansfield

A Note from the Author!

Don't you just love step-mommies? They try extra hard to make little Johnny and Janey love them. They give great presents. They try to make up for the fact that they aren't your real parents.

Sweet.

Unless, of course, they are the wicked witch type of step-mommy.

Then they don't care, and they take hold with a grip of iron and some nasty sex toys and…a gleeful grin.

All of which just goes to show that you shouldn't mess with step-mommy!

STAY HORNY!

Gracie

Part One

"I don't think you understand," said Grant. "When Lucas comes home he is…he's difficult."

He and Shiela were sitting on the second floor balcony, outside the big master bedroom.

He was an older man, sixty, but still had lead in his pencil. His hair was silver, his chin was chiseled, and his eyes were a level grey. Add to that the fact that he did a full work out every day, running, hitting the bag, a little weightlifting, and it was easy to see why a woman twenty years his junior had fallen for him.

Shiela was five foot four, just an inch shorter than Grant, with auburn hair that either hung to her shoulder or was up in a ponytail. Her body was the stuff of dreams. 36 by 24 by 36. But a large 36 on top. Her eyes were blue, the light, opaque kind of blue that was quite good at hiding her thoughts.

"What do you mean by 'difficult?'"

"Well, he's never forgiven me for divorcing his mother."

"So why doesn't he live with her?"

"She won't have him. He's…" he smiled ruefully, "…difficult."

"But if he's difficult with you for divorcing her, why is he difficult with her?"

"That is a question, is it not? For divorcing me?"

Shiela chuckled. She had a low, sultry voice, very sexy, and Grant found himself responding. His pants filled up, his heart started pounding, and… he wanted her.

Unfortunately, while she had proven an easy fuck when they first met, her interest in sex had waned since they had been married.

While his interest had grown. Which is the way it is: you want what you can't have.

"So what's Lucas going to do that will bother me?"

"A sulky attitude. Rudeness. Won't contribute to the house function. That sort of thing."

"So why don't you stop giving him an allowance?

He sighed. "To be honest? Because if I cut him off he just hangs out here, and I'm tired of that."

"All that shouldn't bother me."

"It might, that's why I'm warning you now. I'll be in China, you'll be here, and Lucas might get under your skin."

She smiled and leaned forward. They were in chairs catty corner to each other, and she patted his knee. She had noticed his excitement. "Don't you worry about Mr. Difficult. I know how to handle angry, young men."

"Well, I just thought…"

Her hand rose on his thigh and he started breathing faster.

"You think too much. Want to squirt?"

Oh, Lord, did he!

"I wouldn't mind."

She tugged her chair over, reached into his lap and unzipped him.

"Do you think we could…you know?" He nodded his head back towards the bedroom and the big bed.

"Nah. I like to do it this way."

He acquiesced, sliding down in his chair a little and letting his dingus sprout up.

She gripped him with both hands, she watched him.

His breath caught as her hands moved up and down.

He jerked when she pulled his balls out. He could already feel the sperm roiling around down there.

But he risked it all. "Why don't you want to make love?"

She didn't get mad, like she sometimes did. She just pursed her red lips and studied him. "I don't want to get messy and sweaty. I like watching you when you spew your seed. Most of all, by not letting you top me I retain a certain degree of control. I am my own woman. I am in control."

"Well, I wish you'd let me be in control sometime."

"Now where's the fun in that?" she laughed.

Her hands moved faster, his breath became jerky. He tried to relax, to make it last.

Lord knew he didn't get it enough. Not like before they were married.

She watched him carefully, felt the impulse begin in his testicles, felt the shaft tighten up, throb, and just when he was starting to shoot she slowed down. Gave it a squeeze.

He came, but he only came halfway. His seed spurted a drop, then it drooled half heartedly, then it stopped.

"Oh, fuck!" he wheezed. "Why can't you let me shoot all the way?"

She patted his cheek with her cum wet hand. "Now where would the fun in that be?"

"It would be fun for me," he groused.

"But this way you stay horny. You stay compliant. You give me what I want. You don't treat me like a used up, old wife."

"I wouldn't do that anyway!"

"I don't want to risk it." Then she licked her hand and smiled at him.

He shivered. He still had a load ready to go. Relief was a short-lived thing in their marriage.

Later that night, when Grant was asleep in bed, Shiela got up and wandered through the house.

She wore a pale blue negligee over her thrusting tits. She kept it open so her pussy was visible. She carried a small drawstring pouch in one hand.

There was nobody to see her, but she still liked to act like there was.

She was an exhibitionist always on parade. Always showing off her spectacular body. Always sexy and sultry.

She didn't get turned on by sex, she got turned on by denying sex.

Having a man dripping in her hand, unable to get the rest of it out, was the biggest turn on in her life.

She went out to the pool and sat in a lounge chair under the eaves.

She was under the bedroom and the moonlight shone directly on her, but even if Grant was awake he wouldn't be able to see her.

She sighed and felt like the moonlight was illuminating her every secret.

And her every secret was that she was loveless. She had married for money. She didn't want to fuck the old man.

But his son…hmmm. That might be interesting.

She was 40, Lucas was 20, and she was a MILF in the truest sense of the word.

Young men made her hot, made her wet. Just thinking about them was a thrill. Their strong, young bodies. Their stiff penises. The way they looked at her, lusted after her, thinking they could never hope to get between her thighs.

But they could. And did. And mostly it was her doing the come on.

And Lucas was due home.

In fact, she was going to take Grant to the airport, send him off for a couple of months, and pick up Lucas within an hour.

Out with the old, in with the new.

Perfect.

She sighed in the moonlight, her large breasts heaving, her negligee falling apart and revealing her triangle.

She had her hair removed long ago. It didn't even grow back now, and she loved to sit and feel her soft mons, her fleshy labia, her pointed clitoris.

She had nipple rings, and once she had had rings through her labia.

Maybe she should do that again. Get a nice big set of rings for men to grip and pull apart and reveal her wet pinkness.

Maybe while Grant was away. Yes. Get her labia pierced, maybe introduce Mr. Difficult Lucas to a little kinky sex.

He would want her as a MILF, everybody did. But to want her as a kink. To put some screws in the basement wall, some eye-screws. To chain her nipples to the wall, to wear chains on her upper thighs and keep her labia open and dripping.

She was hot now, just thinking about what could be done to her.

She opened the drawstring bag and took out a pink vibrator. A small one with a bulb on one end and a thin handle on the other. She arched her back and inserted the pink vibrator into her anus.

The sensations rocketed through her. She shivered, up the body, like a dog shaking off water.

She took out a glass dildo, one with a slight bend and a ball on the end. She pressed it to her mons, ran it up and down her slit, and quake with desire.

That was the thing: ruining Grant's orgasms made her so horny she couldn't stand it.

But what if she didn't have the boy do nasty things to her…what if she did them to him?

She had done that a couple of times. She had taken a young man once, tied him to a bed and striped his ass. She had stuffed a dildo in his mouth, put a chastity tube on him, and teased him 24/7 for a week.

Until she could no longer stand up.

She had gone to bed, him crying out for her, humping the air and begging, and when she came back to him, after a good night's sleep, he was goofy.

He was like a moron, babbling and drooling and begging for sex.

She hadn't, of course, let him have any. She had simply let him loose and showed him the door.

He hung around the front, and she called the police.

And while he cried and sobbed and begged for a fuck, a stick up his ass, a kiss…she had had some of the best solo sessions of her life.

She had a spent a week doing nothing but getting herself off. While he wandered the streets, hid in the bushes and jacked—before the police picked him up—and wasn't worth much after that.

Hunh! He had been a law student with promise, until he met her. Last she heard he was standing in lines at soup kitchens.

Lucas was coming home.

Hmmm.

The next morning Shiela rolled over and stroked Grant for a long while. She edged him, then she kissed him and got up.

He whined and made gulping noises.

She took a shower.

Then she hopped into the Mercedes and trucked on down to the tattoo parlor

'Ink You!' was the name on the building, and the windows were blacked out.

Inside the building were three chairs, no waiting. The walls had artwork on them. The place smelled of ink, that peculiar smell, and there were two fellows sitting in the chairs, feet up, smoking cigarettes.

They both had sleeves. They were both bearded, and one had nipple rings. The other one had rings in his ears, big rings.

One of them started to stand up but Shiela just motioned him down.

The artists were bemused as she walked around them, then she chose the one on the right. "I've had rings in my pussy before, four on each labia, and I want them again. I want the minimum bleeding, I'm in a hurry to… do things."

"The man on the left stood up. "Let's go in the back."

They went in the back because they didn't want Shiela laying with her legs open in the front. which was odd because that would have been nothing but good advertisement for a place like theirs.

The back had one chair with legs that separated, straps to hold the legs, or arms, or whatever, in place. People moving while needles were poking through their privates, or whatever, were an invitation to disaster.

"How thick?"

"Thick."

He held up a series of rings, one at a time, until she chose a set.

She hadn't worn panties, but she had them in her purse, in case of blood.

She lifted her skirt and hopped up on the chair.

It was comfortable, nicely cushioned, and the man got to work.

"This will be easy," he said. "The marks are still there."

"Bleeding?"

"Not much. Probably not at all, but don't sue me if there is blood."

"Hell! If there's blood then I just won't fuck you."

He grinned. He could tell that Miss High Falutin was serious. He would be extra careful.

Slowly he put a needle through her soft flesh, Everything went smoothly, and within half an hour she was adorned. She had four big, thick rings on each lip, and there was no blood.

He held a mirror for here while she was in the chair and she examined his work and nodded.

"Nice. Want to fuck me now?"

He did.

She got home an hour later, just in time to take Grant to the airport.

"Where you been?" he asked cheerfully as he rolled his big suitcase through the house.

"Got some rings put in my pussy."

He stopped and blinked and turned to her. He didn't say anything, just looked at her.

He was used to her quirks and idiosyncrasies, but this…rings in her pussy?

She lifted her skirt and spread her legs and tilted her hips out. The rings pushed out, an even set of four on a side, and her moistness made a silvery sparkle.

His mouth dropped open.

"Something for you to dream about while you're in China."

"Oh, Lord," he whispered, smacking his lips.

"Just think. I'll be sampling every dildo I can, and when you get back I'm going to put a lock on the rings. You won't be able to get your dick in me. You'll like that, won't you?"

"I'd like to get in you," he whispered, mesmerized by her rings.

"Too bad, so sad," she dropped her skirt. "Now pack the car and let's go."

Five minutes later they were driving to the airport. She was driving. He was staring at her, his pants bulging out, a bit of drool actually leaking from his mouth.

"So Lucas is trouble," she commented.

Sighing, his eyes on her crotch, his imagination on her rings, he said, "He can be. He's a sensitive boy, at least he was. He was actually sort of a mama's boy. then he grew up and became resentful."

"Before the divorce?"

"A little bit before, a lot after."

"Well, I'll handle him."

"How?" he asked, genuinely curious.

"I'll empty the basement, make a dungeon out of it. I'll use whips and sex to cow him. I'll train him."

This was hard talk, and while Shiela was a bit of a wild hair, this was even wilder.

Then he thought: *fuck it!*

"Well, if that's what it takes, you have my permission."

"Honey!" She grinned at him as she held the wheel. "I don't need your permission."

He had to laugh then.

"What's got into you?" he asked.

"I don't know. I'm just feeling a little…crazy. Maybe it's all that sex you've been denying me."

"I denied you?" He shook his head and laughed lightly. "Don't you think it's the other way around?"

"Are you kidding?"

She reached over and grabbed his hand, she pulled it across the console and placed it on her right tit.

He could feel her nipple, hot, pointed, and her blood pulsing in her breast.

"Honey, you get me so horny that I have to masturbate all the time. When you're sleeping, when you're at work, all the time. While you're shuffling papers or counting sheep I've got a vibrator up my pussy and I'm working it like a hockey player works his stick."

Now Grant's cock was ready to burst. He had only had half a cum the day before, and that made him hornier.

But before he could do anything Shiela pulled into the airport.

Grant stepped out of the car and he was half bent over courtesy of his hard cock.

Shiela stepped out and grinned as he shuffled, half bent, to the trunk and got out his luggage.

They walked together, and slowly his hard on waned.

"Not going to miss me, eh?" She 'accidentally' brushed a hand against his groin.

He groaned, and his pecker started up again.

"Honey. We're going to have to have a long talk when I get home."

"Or a long fuck. Which did you want? A talk or a fuck? Both are four letter words."

He shook his head, actually a bit out of sorts with all this odd and highly charged tension.

She walked him to the gate, stood with him for a few moments and watched the big airliners roll up to the gates.

"Here we go," he mumbled, watching a ground crew scurry about.

The big tube with wings rolled up and the walkway was rolled up tot he door.

"Okay, honey. I love you."

"I love you, too," she lied, kissing his cheek. "And don't worry about Lucas."

He chuckled. "A dungeon, eh? If only it was that simple."

Then they hugged and he was gone.

She didn't bother watching the plane leave, those things would sit around forever, gassing up and loading luggage. Instead, she headed for the airport bar.

"Death in the Afternoon," she stated to the bartender. He was trying to eye her boobs surreptitiously, and not doing a good job of it. "And if you don't take your eyes off my boobs I'll throw it in your face."

He kept his eyes off her boobs and served her the drink.

It came in a flute. It was milky white, a combination of absinthe and champagne. Some people said it was sweet, and some said it tasted like licorice. Whatever, it gave a high that was almost hallucinogenic.

"Another one," she commanded, sipping at the first. When he brought the second one she decided to reward him. After all, him staring at her boobs was a compliment, and he had fetched the drinks speedily.

"Sorry I was snappy. But men with big dicks always make me that way."

He gulped and his eyes actually fluttered. but he tried to be around and helpful as she sipped the second drink.

Shiela turned and watched out the doors, out the big windows, and waited for Lucas to arrive.

He was coming in on Southwest, and she was in a perfect position to check out the planes as they taxied up.

She watched, ordered another Death in the Afternoon, and counted jets.

Five jets matched the arrival board, and she stood up and walked out of the bar.

The barman stared after her wistfully. What an ass! What tits! what a bitch!

Shiela had never met Lucas, nor him her. But she had seen a picture of him. Unfortunately, the picture was taken some years previously, and he had changed.

She stood across the corridor from the gate and watched people exit the plane.

Fat, old lady, kids, lots of businessmen. A few lovers. If parting brings sweet sorrow, then joining must bring sorrowful sweet. Right?

She watched a gaggle of girls get off the plane. A skinny kid with skanky hair and a frowse of beard. Nothing like the picture of the sweet high school freshman.

The plane empty, Shiela wandered down to the baggage pick up. There was still half a crowd there, and a few people that looked out to the pick up area.

Nobody that resembled Lucas.

But the scruffy, skinny kid who slumped and wore sunglasses indoors was there. With his bags, and suddenly Shiela recognized his bags. They looked like Grant's, like they were from the same set.

She walked up behind the kid, looked down at his ass. Huh. Same sort of ass as Grant. A little slack.

The set of the shoulders was the same, though slumped a bit.

But she knew.

"Hello, Lucas."

He turned, lifted his head slightly to look under his sunglasses at her, and grunted. "I've been waiting."

"Tough shit you little shit."

She could tell that he blinked behind his glasses. The crink of the skin at the corners of his eyes, the slight bob of his head. Yep. He had blinked.

"Follow me."

She turned and strode off, towards the parking area, and he was faced with the fact of having to hurry up and catch up while hauling his bags.

She walked fast, making him hurry more. She stopped as she came to the horse shoe shaped drive, and waited for a light.

He caught up to her. "Are you Shiela?"

"No," she answered, just to be spiteful. Just to fuck with his head.

"Then who are you?"

She didn't answer, just crossed the street and started angling through the parking area.

They reached the Mercedes and she used her fob to pop the trunk.

He put his bags in the trunk, and kept watching her.

She got into the driver's seat and waited for him. When he was seated she started the car.

"Then who are you."

"Shiela."

"What the fuck?" Surliness raised its ugly head again. "What the fuck is it with you?"

He certainly wasn't cowed by her beauty, and she sort of liked that.

"So, your dad said you were an asshole, and I'm here to say that that won't fly."

"Fuck you."

"That's it. You won't unless your straighten up and fly right."

He figured it out, and for the first time his mouth opened a little, revealed the simple mind behind all the insults. "What?"

They came to the ticket booth and she stopped the car and waited for the

Chevy in front of them to stop talking and get moving. She turned to him and said in a clear voice. "I said, if you do everything I say I'll fuck the shit out of you. If you don't, then I'll poison your soup, take a baseball bat to your ass, and I don't mean sideways, and you will remember, all your life, of the opportunity you missed."

He was silent for a while after that.

She pulled her skirt up and revealed her rings.

As she moved her hips the rings gave a couple of tinkles, and Lucas stared, and now his mouth was open.

"You like?"

He nodded.

"Then you can have…if you follow certain conditions."

"What conditions."

She thought about telling him. Thought about revealing that she was going to leave his father. Just empty his bank accounts, and leave, but… but she wanted to do more.

Because there was a mean streak in her.

She wanted to leave Grant a gift that was better, or worse, than money.

And who better than his dopey son.

She decided not to tell him. Heck, he might prove contrary if he knew what she was thinking about doing.

"That's for me to know and you to suck eggs."

He was blinking. The city was passing. The motor was humming.

"Can you get down here and eat my pussy?"

"Uh…"

"I said—"

"I heard what you said!"

"Then get your dopey head down here and get to work."

He undid his seat buckle and leaned over the console. It was awkward, she had to hold the wheel with her hands up and her elbows out of the way.

His head was having trouble pushing deep enough, and finally he just stuck his finger in her.

"Hey!" she screeched, and she slapped him on the back of the head.

He straightened up, rubbed the back of his head, but damned if there wasn't a smirky sort of half grin on his stupid face!

"God," she said in disgust.

He just sat back and grinned.

They arrived home and she pulled the Mercedes into the driveway. She got out and strode away, her high heels clicking noisily and powerfully.

Lucas got out his luggage and walked into the house.

His mind was actually in a bit of a daze.

Yes, he had gotten her, sort of, with his finger, but now that that was over he was thinking about her pussy. About the rings. About the soft, wet feel of her vagina.

So she was going to fuck him, eh? Sounded like a head trip. She wanted to be a dominatrix, or something.

Well, she might qualify for that. The pony tail look was powerful, and her ass had certainly been a trip when she walked up the walk to the house.

And she had those mighty tits and that red lipstick.

But he wasn't in to being bullied.

He hadn't had many girlfriends. Under his sullen exterior he was sullen, and he never had much luck with girls, so he was bitter, too.

Sullen and bitter. Not a good combination for getting a girlfriend.

He took his bags to the room above the garage, which was his.

It was a big room, big as a garage, and he had a bed, a gaming station, a pool table, and books. Lots of books. Especially books by Grace Mansfield.

She was the one, in his universe.

And that was one more reason why he never had a girlfriend. He was waiting for a woman, a strong woman, maybe even like Shiela, to take him in hand, to dress him up, to bring him to heel.

One more reason to be sulky.

He rolled his suitcase into a corner and flopped on the bed.

Shiela walked in. Naked. Her pony tail now squarely on top of her head, her hair pulled tight, her lipstick fresh and shiny. Her tits shook as she walked, and his mouth opened in surprise. She had a coiled length of something over her shoulder.

"What the fuck—OW!"

She snapped the whip across his belly.

He rolled over the side of the bed and cowered, and looked up at her as she rounded the bed.

"What I say goes!" CRACK!

He scrambled over the bed and she caught him on the ass. CRACK!

He cried out and lurched and darted into the bathroom. He slammed the door and braced against it.

"Come out of there, you little shit!"

"No!" He was crying now.

"Then you better be clean, and clean shaven, your hair brushed out, in one hour. I'll be back."

The sound of her walking, then heels clicking on the stairs, then… silence.

Lucas walked over to the mirror. His belly had a stripe on it, and his butt had a short mark. Damn!

He took a wash cloth and ran cold water over it, then he thought, *fuck it.*

He stepped into the shower. He let cold water run on his ass, then his belly, then he turned the temperature up.

Heysoos, he thought. *What is with that bitch!*

In the back of his mind was that fact that she had given him an hour.

The hour passed, and he was clean, but his hair was a scraggle, and he still had the rubble of face hair.

She appeared in his doorway.

Naked. Big tits. Those damned rings tinkling between her thighs. This time she was smiling and holding a little jar.

"How you doing, Lucas?"

"I'm fine," he said with suspicion. Was this some kind of good cop bad cop thing?

She came to his bed and held up the jar. "Ointment, for your wounds. But you have to get undressed.

He wasn't too dressed to begin with, just a towel, but he didn't intend to get naked for her.

Even though his boner started poking up the towel.

She grabbed the edge of the towel and pulled.

"Hey!"

She straddled him, her pussy, and its rings, against his cock, but not on it. The rings were hard and weird. Her pussy was wet.

"That was certainly mean of me," she said as she dipped a finger and spread cold ointment on the stripe on his belly.

"Yeah. What the fuck."

She nodded, then simply said, "It's your choice. I can whip you until you follow orders, or you can follow orders and get a little pleasure."

"What kind of pleasure?"

"I told you. A good fuck."

"But you're my dad's wife!"

"So?"

And the seeds were sown.

Every man competes, on some level, with his father.

Every man wants his mother. That's basic oedipus rex.

But she wasn't his mother.

She was his step-mother, and that was a whole different bag of cats.

He could fuck his father's wife. His fake mother. And his dick rose up, strong and powerful.

Shiela smiled. "I see you're thinking now. Would you like a sample?"

"Fuck you?"

For answer she rose up, and settled half down.

He could feel her softness, her wetness, her heat. She reached down and pulled on the rings, opened up her pussy, and he stared down at the sight of his cock half sliding into the pink.

He about shot his load right then, but she pulled off.

"All you have to do is shave, brush your hair. Heck, I'll brush your hair, and you can have some more of that. If you're real good you might get a lot of that."

He made a 'gurking' sound and looked up at her face.

Sheila had a wonderful face. For a mean person she had a soft, compassionate face. Her lips so large and red, her eyes so expressive.

But even if she had had a mean face, he was getting so riled up he would have thought her face was sweet.

She leaned down, her breasts heavy on his chest, the nipples poking into him.

Her face was an inch away from his, their lips close, their breath mingling.

"Try it, Lucas. Try it my way. Let's clean you up, make you beautiful. Let's see what we can do. You do for me, and I'll do for you. And you know what that means."

"It means I get to fuck you."

"It means you get to put your penis in me. Whether you will get to do a full fuck, that is something you'll have to earn. Whether you get to cum...I don't know. That depends on how well you treat me."

Then she said something that blew his mind.

"I like pretty, little girls. Will you be a pretty, little girl for me?"

He stared, his eyes big and open, his heart was pounding and his mind was tipping over into crazyland. She leaned further.

Their lips met and he had never felt anything so soft and gentle and beautiful and...and his cock would have erupted, except that she was holding it by the base.

Part Two

Grant's plane was landing in Hawaii by the time Shiela had Lucas in a shower.

Lucas was slathered with Nair and his skin was burning. He watched in fascination as his hair swirled down the drain.

His dingus was at full strength.

She was going to feminize him!

He stood, shivering in spite of the heat of the water, and couldn't believe the sensations coursing through his body.

"Come on, Lucas!" Shiela opened the door and held a towel for him.

Lucas stepped out and she began rubbing his body. He just stood there and she dried his chest off, and sucked on his nipples. She dried his legs, and kissed his cock while she was down there. She dried his arms and kissed his lips. She led him, by the cock, to her vanity table. She sat him down and began brushing his hair, trimming it, layering it and giving it. a feminine appearance.

He stared at himself in the mirror.

He wore his hair with no concern. It was frowzy and unkempt. As long as a woman's hair, but never styled because, well, because he was shy. Call it embarrassed.

Now she was shaping it around his face, down over his shoulders, emphasizing his soft, brown eyes.

He could hardly breath.

And every once in a while she would just stop and stare at him in the mirror, her fingers tickling his nipples, his cock standing straight out.

"Why didn't you do this yourself…a long time ago."

"I…I was scared."

"Scared of being beautiful? You silly goose."

She took a hair dryer to him and mussed his hair, and it gained a full body. The shampoo and conditioner she had made him use gave his locks a sheen that was really quite spectacular.

Done, his hair full, his body clean and hairless, including his chin, she stood him up.

"I can't stand it," she murmured. She put him on the bed, tied him face down, a pillow under his cock so he wouldn't bend it, and so…his ass was elevated.

"What are you doing?" he asked.

She bent to her side table and opened the lowest drawer. He couldn't see over the edge of the bed, but she lifted an object up and he stared at it.

It was silver, bulbous, and had a blue jewel in the end. She sat next to him on the bed and put it to his mouth.

"Suck this, and suck it good."

Dutifully, so excited that now he couldn't refuse her even if he wanted to, he opened his mouth and took the butt plug in.

"This is made out of metal. It's heavy and it will cause a bit of…shall we call it 'drag?'—on your butt hole. It will feel so incredibly good, and you'll wish it was bigger. And all I can say to that is…be patient."

He sucked, his eyes big as he watched her.

He was tied down, but he wished he wasn't. He wanted to be on top of her, even though she had sort of indicated that that might not happen.

She took the plug from his mouth and slid down to his butt. She pulled his cheeks apart and pushed the thing into him.

The bulb was rough going through the ring, and he gasped, but the pain was quick and then over with.

It felt like heaven!

He felt full, complete, like there was a ball of lightening in his butt. He had thought his cock was stiff before, but that was nothing. Now it was like a tire iron, but ten times fatter!

And it was throbbing, the blood rushing through it like a raging river filled with snow melt.

hot snow melt.

He lay there, making gurking sounds, and she inspected her work thoughtfully.

He was hairless, which was quite sexy to her. She wasn't a fan of hairy beasts. He had hair that would be the envy of women everywhere.

But it was his butt that fascinated her.

She had had anal sex, on the receiving end. She liked it. Sometimes it was even better than vaginal sex.

But now she was looking down at his plugged up butt and thinking about being on the giving end.

What would it feel like to take a dildo to those wonderful depths? What would it be like to play where the sun didn't shine?

The thoughts were exciting, and suddenly she was breathing as hard as Lucas.

What if she did it to him?

No, she wouldn't feel anything in her penis, because she didn't have one. But she would feel that excitement in her chest, that satisfaction of taking true charge.

What if she did him?

She sighed, and rubbed his buns with her hands. Squeezing, manipulating, pushing his buns together and pulling them apart.

That she was creating quite an effect in him was obvious. He was groaning and pushing his ass up, and when she pressed on the blue jewel, and wiggled the handle, he moaned like an orgasm.

But, of course, he wasn't having an orgasm. And she was't about to allow him one.

She grinned. But getting him close, and denying him, that was the equivalent of an orgasm for her.

She suddenly stood up, then laid down next to him, on her side and facing him.

"How's that feel, sweet cheeks?"

"Umm." his eyes were glazed. He was aware, sexually aware of her, but he was focused on his butt. The world was being filtered through his asshole.

"I need to give you a spanking."

"What…what for?" A spark of fear in his chocolate eyes.

"For all the bad things you've ever done."

He had no idea what she was talking about, but he blubbered, "But I'm sorry! You don't have to...to..."

She shushed him with a gentle kiss, enjoyed the fear in him, and whispered, "Of course I do."

He was trying to catch his breath, but couldn't.

She got off the bed and walked into Grant's closet. She came out with a thick, leather belt. She folded it, held the ends and brought her hands together, then pulled them apart.

SPLAT! The belt smacked against itself.

"Oh, fuck," whimpered Lucas.

"I'll be gentle this first time," she promised.

SMACK!

"OW!"

She leaned down to him. "Shhh. If you get too loud I'll put a penis gag in your mouth. Learn a little self control, a little discipline. Don't abuse my delicate ears."

She backed up and smacked him again.

SMACK!

He groaned, and it was load for a groan, but it was soft for a yell.

Good, she thought. *He's trying!*

SMACK! SMACK! SMACK!

She struck softer, she varied the strokes, the timing. She watched as he tried to push down into the mattress, in spite of the obstacle created by his stiff dick.

She thought it was quite funny that he looked like he was trying to fuck the mattress.

she struck near his plug, but never directly on it. That would have been too much.

Then she was done. She went back to the closet and hung the belt up.

Lucas was crazed. The pain had been unbelievable at first, then when she started changing the strokes on him, the pain became...something else.

Not quite pleasure, it still hurt, but...something else.

He was unaware of the effects of the chemicals released by his addled brain. He didn't know about endorphins regulating the amount of pain he perceived. And he certainly didn't understand that at a certain point pain becomes pleasure.

Not great pleasure, but that was coming. Shiela did understand about endorphins, and she knew that she had ignited them, but had not overloaded him. And now it was time for the real treat.

She left the room, headed for the kitchen, and Lucas lay there, breathing hard, wondering what was going on.

Shiela returned a minute later, and she was holding a small cup. In it she had mixed three kitchen ingredients.

"I should have taken the time to make sure the proportions were proper. But this will do it." she began smoothing a paste onto his burning rump, and the burning started to increase!

"This is capsaicin, from chili peppers, piperine from black pepper, and gingerol, from ginger. Normally you wouldn't feel them, by themselves they are pretty mild, but I've opened up your pores. You're going to feel the heat now, honey."

She rubbed the mixture against his flesh, smushed it into his skin, and the burning sensation got worse and worse. Or better and better, depending on your viewpoint.

"Oh, God! That's hot!" He wiggled, and now Shiela gripped the base of his plug and held it.

The effect was of him wiggling, and fucking the plug. She didn't wiggle it, he did, he fucked himself against her plug holding hand.

She giggled as his ass turned red and he screwed up against her hand.

He moaned and tried to twist out from under the burning sensation.

It wasn't terrible, but in conjunction with the spanking he had just received, it was making him uncomfortable. but in a weirdly pleasant way.

For ten minutes they stayed there, him wiggling, her letting him screw himself, then he just collapsed.

He was overloaded. He still burned, but...there was nothing he could do about it, and then Shiela noticed something.

"Oh, you bad boy! You came!"

He didn't know that. He was just exhausted, burned, and in a strangely sexual haze of…satisfaction.

"You rubbed your prostate against the plug and drained your own semen!"

He sighed. Good. He was happy. He felt like he had just had an orgasm, though he hadn't.

She reached under him. His penis was soft. Yep, he had drained himself.

"Well, we can't have that."

"Unh!" he grunted. Smiling.

She reached into her drawer once again. She loosened one leg and twisted him half over. She pulled his cock and balls through a ring, then she placed a tube on his cock.

"What's that?" he smiled, ready to sleep.

"It's something to make sure you don't get too rambunctious. Now, listen," she said as she clicked a little lock shut, "I don't like you cumming. But what you did, that's actually all right. The problem is that you did it without permission."

"Why is it all right?"

"Because in a short while you will be hornier than before. Your body squirted, but your brain doesn't know it. In a few minutes you will be hornier, harder, and quite desperate. That, I like."

She undid his other restraints and helped him sit up.

He looked down at his poor, caged cock.

His cock had room in the chastity tube. But he felt a strange sensation. He felt a heat inside, a desire, like he had a boner, but…he didn't have one.

"You already feel it, don't you?"

He looked up at her. "My butt is hurting again."

"Your butt is hurting, your cock is trying to get erect, but…too bad, so sad." She smiled, grabbed his hair on both sides of his head and kissed him. But this time she didn't kiss and release.

She held him there, their lips fused together, and she opened her eyes and watched him.

He felt his penis struggling then, trying to get erect, and she let go with one hand and held his pectoral muscle like it was a boob.

His ass started burning harder, his cock was now hurting, and still she held him.

Lip to lip, eye to eye, absorbing the sexual implications of his pain.

He finally pulled back, gasped for breath. "What are you doing?"

"Enjoying you. Come on, let's get you dressed."

She pulled him off the bed and he stood there rubbing his ass. "Can I wash my ass off?"

"Sure. It's in your pores now, it'll be hours before the sensations go away."

He went into the bathroom and rubbed his ass with a cold wash cloth. Then he rubbed soap in an effort to clean himself of the burning chemicals on his butt. If anything that made it worse.

When he came out, tears in his eyes, she remarked happily, "Did you know there are soaps in napalm?"

He groaned and rubbed his ass again.

"The best cure is just to leave it alone until it dissipates."

She was laughing on the inside. Sure, he would leave it alone, and that was the cure, but he would be wiggling and squirming until it wore off.

She handed him a bra. She had cut the cups out and it was just a frame, but it fit him perfectly.

"We'll get you some hormones, or maybe some implants. Then you'll need a complete bra. But, right now, let's just train you in wearing one."

She adjusted straps and he stood and looked down at his pectorals and his nipples.

He didn't have much in the way of boobs, but the bra framework emphasized what he did have, and that made his cock struggle even harder.

She reached down and shook his caged cock and his knees grew weak. "Oh, please," he moaned.

"Sure." She let go of him, and he was sorry. He liked the feeling of her hand on him.

She handed him panties and helped him pull them up tight. They were stretchy and even had a pouch. They were sissy panties that she had bought once, then realized her mistake, but she still had them, and they fit him perfectly.

He looked at himself in the mirror, was struck at how feminine his body looked even with these accouterments on.

"I should have been born a girl," he said.

She handed him nylons, put him on the bed—he winced as his heat addled buns felt the cool, soft sheets—and helped him put them on.

And high heels. He was a few inches shorter than her, and had small feet for a man. The shoes fit him perfectly, and now he not only felt his burning ass, but his ankles wobbled almost uncontrollably.

She sat him on the chair in front of her vanity table and giggled as he wiggled. "Sit still," she admonished, and she began working on his face.

Cleansing his pores, primer, foundation, she prepared him for the art.

She put on blush, matched his tones and hues, then began working on his eyes.

He stared at the mirror, trying not to move as his ass burned. She felt his 'boobs,' and smiled, and shadowed his eyelids.

She gripped his cage and shook it fiercely, causing him to move on the chair and irritate his butt, and coated his lips with plumper and painted them a bright red.

She outlined his eyes, added mascara, and he stared at the sharp point of the little pencil so close to his eyes.

He was beautiful.

He was like a little Ladyboy from Thailand. A lady boy with small boobs and a big cock.

Except that the big cock was trapped inside the chastity tube.

A lady boy who she wanted to lay down and...do things to.

She sighed in satisfaction, seeing the beauty she had created.

Lucas, in spite of the burning of his ass (it wasn't quite as bad now, the chemicals were finally wearing off), sighed in satisfaction.

This was what he wanted.

Grant was just landing in China.

Shiela held a leash, and the leash went to the end of Lucas's cock cage. She strode through the house imperiously. She went into the backyard, and he followed, and made the little whining sounds she loved so much.

She sat and sunbathed, no clothing, and she made him fan her with a big palm leaf.

Lucas loved it. He was in a permanent haze of pounding sexuality. His cock was trying to hard to get hard it hurt. The more he did, the more she demanded of him...the more he submitted, the more he wanted to submit.

She lay on the lounge chair, told him to get her a drink, and while he was gone she thought about what was next.

So much to do, so little time.

Breasts, hormones, a dungeon. Whippings, maybe some piercings.

Yes, piercings.

She did so enjoy her own rings. they way they jangled when she walked, the way she could pull her labia apart, expose her inner workings, before she slid down Lucas's hefty cock.

Of course, now that she had him caged, she probably wouldn't be sliding down him anymore. At least, not until she was ready to drain him again.

And that was the problem.

Draining often resulted in a harder cock, one that wouldn't cum, one that could be sat upon safely without having to worry about the mess.

But, sometimes, like the last, and first, time she had drained Lucas, which had been strictly by accident, he had grown soft.

If she fucked him he would cum in her. But if she drained him he might not be hard enough to provide her with his stiff and uncummable penis.

So how much could she drain him and be sure he wouldn't squirt, and yet still retain a stiff ding dong?

That was the problem.

Lucas arrived back with a Long Island Tea.

Shiela had spent a bit of time training the boy on how to make a proper Long Island Tea. The formula itself, without even getting into the mixing, was daunting.

    3/4 ounce vodka

    3/4 ounce white rum

3/4 ounce silver tequila

3/4 ounce gin

3/4 ounce triple sec

3/4 ounce simple syrup

3/4 ounce lemon juice, freshly squeezed

Cola, to top

Garnish: lemon wedge

Fortunately, the boy learned well. The drink was delicious and she commanded him to go get her lipstick.

He ran, and she sipped, and when he got back she freshened his mouth, and her own.

Then he fanned her with the palm leaf, she sipped and luxuriated, and thought about his future.

Precisely, she thought about his ass.

It was red, but had stopped hurting. She would have to fix that again. She loved to make her boytoys uncomfortable; she loved a butt that wiggled helplessly.

And that brought her to the real crux of the matter.

She had him in a butt plug. He was plugged up solid.

But she wanted more.

Heck, he wanted to be a girl, and there was more to being a girl than simply make up.

There was…sex.

But was he up for that?

To look at him, the common observation would be not.

But she had a feeling. She had a feeling deep in her gut that he was not just ready, he was craving.

He had admitted to her that he had often dreamed of being a woman.

Had he dreamed of having sex the way a woman does?

Probably. Likely. But…there was only one way to find out.

"Lucas. Go up to my bedside drawer, the one with the toys in it, and bring me back the flesh colored dildo."

He put the palm leaf aside and dashed away.

She could hear him, trying to run in his high heels, as he ran down the hallway and into her bedroom.

She imagined him looking into the drawer, and she grinned.

Upstairs Lucas pulled the drawer open and gasped.

It was a large drawer, deep down and deep back, and it was filled with toys.

There were vibrators and dildos, butt plugs and a TENS unit. There were penis gags and various types of restraints. There were chastity tubes with spikes on the inside, and he shivered.

He rummaged through the drawer and found a six inch long dildo. Flesh colored.

He closed the drawer and ran back through the house, almost falling as he made his way clumsily down the stairs.

He slowed down, worked on clicking his heels on the patio, and handed Shiela the dildo.

"Turn around."

He turned.

"Bend over."

He bent, and now his mind was a riot. What was she going to do to him?

She pulled down his stretchy sissy panties and extracted the blue jeweled butt plug. She put it on the table her drink was on, and sucked on the dildo for a moment. She sucked, her red lips going back and forth on the shaft, spreading saliva all over it.

She pressed it into him. Gently. A wiggle here and a waggle there.

He gasped, but he held his position.

It went in, in, and Lucas sobbed with pleasure.

He felt the latex balls nudge up against his own balls. Then she turned the dildo, turned it inside him, and it was all he could do not to straighten up.

"Oh, fuck!" he whimpered, his insides heating up with excitement and a curious satisfaction.

He had played with his butt before. He had even put small things up there. Small bottles with short necks. but this was different!

This was a real penis! Well, a plastic penis, but it was the correct size! It was very like the real thing!

It reached full depth, filled him completely. His anal ring was stretched out, his balls were tight and his penis had never tried so hard to be erect!

Shiela moved it around, and he couldn't stop a guttural moan from coming out of his mouth.

She moved it in and out, just an inch, slowly building up the force. Going a little faster, smacking it into him.

He began to drain.

She pulled it out of him.

He actually fell down, across the lounge chair next to Shiela's

Shiela stared at his gaping hole. Yes. He was ready. He was more than ready.

"Lucas, as soon as you can walk, go make a couple more Long Island Teas."

Lucas couldn't speak, but he could nod, be it slowly.

It took a couple of minutes, his muscles had been frozen in the bent over position, but he straightened up. Slowly. Like an old man. Like an old man who had been fucked by a dildo.

He walked, stumbling, uncoordinated, back into the house.

Inside the house he slowly regained the ability to breath naturally.

He felt good. So good. He felt even more complete than when she had put the butt plug into him.

And now that he had had a dick-sized object, a life-sized plastic peter, inside him, he realized that he walked funny, and that he would likely forever walk funny.

He had been opened up.

It reminded him of how some gay men walked, of how they 'swished,' when they walked.

He wasn't gay, he was still turned on by girls, especially by Shiela, but he loved the feeling of being impacted up the poop chute.

If God hadn't wanted men to fill their fannies he wouldn't have made their assholes so like vaginas.

Right?

He made a pair of Long Island Teas, paid attention scrupulously to the formula, then brought the drinks back out to the patio.

He handed Shiela hers, then sat down on the lounge chair next to her. He hadn't been told to, but…his legs were almost collapsing under him. He needed to.

His ass didn't burn, but it was tender. His hole felt…different. He wiggled, but for a different reason. He wanted that dildo back up his heinie.

Shiela drank, and watched him.

"We're going to make love."

"We are?"

He brightened up, but not as much as he normally would have. But he wasn't as excited by the thought of putting his penis into Shiela as he was of having a penis fill his backside.

But not a man's penis! I'm not gay! I just like…like girly things. And if taking a penis in your hole wasn't girl he didn't know what was.

Shiela smiled and cut through his confusion and reassured him. "But it's not you fucking me, it's me fucking you."

He became brighter, and she saw it.

"So drink your drink, then we will go upstairs and I will introduce you to real love making, the way a woman does it.

A Long Island Tea is a potent drink, and Shiela actually had him make a few more, but then they walked upstairs, her holding the leash to his cage and her pussy rings jingling.

She unhooked the leash in the bedroom and told him to sit on the bed.

He sat, and watched as she placed a harness around her waist and buckled it. She screwed a big, black dildo—much bigger than the one she had left laying on the patio—onto her strap on harness.

She stood in front of him. She lifted him and kissed him mercilessly. She pushed him down and made him suck her dick. She pushed him over on the bed and moved up behind him.

Then she said the strangest thing. "This is for your father," and she rode him.

Rode him like a cheap ass mule, slapping his hot buttocks, reaching around and pinching his nipples, grabbing his cage and twisting it until he yelped.

But, as rough as she was, or maybe because of how rough she was, he loved it.

He moaned. He cried out in pleasure. He pushed back and fucked her dildo.

He drained all over the bed and down the side of it. A thick stream of clumpy sperm. The proof of his love and lust.

And it was as good as she thought it would be. No, she didn't feel anything down there, but her chest exploded with the pride of ownership. She wallowed in the fact that he was hers, a possession to be used as she wished.

It was power, and now she had it better than she had ever imagined.

An hour she pulled back. His back was bruised where she had slapped him and struck him. His butt was bright red with her brutality. But he was empty. And as happy as he had ever been.

He felt like a real man.

And she felt better than a real man.

My Step-Mommy Feminized Me!
Bondage and BDSM? Really?

Grace Mansfield

A Note from the Author!

This is actually a sequel to 'The Feminizing Step-Mother!'

Shiela is tired of marriage, and now she's had her husband's son by a previous marriage foisted upon her.

But Shiela is not about to put up with it. Her tools are feminization, her weapons are BDSM and Bondage.

And her goal is to get rich!

STAY HORNY!
Gracie

Part One

The problem was that Shiela didn't have enough connections to make happen what she needed to happen. She did, however, have enough money.

She had a step-son, Lucas, who would acquiesce to the changes she wished for.

Her husband, Grant, was gone to China for a couple of months.

So there was nothing standing in her way…except herself.

While Lucas slept upstairs…well, he wasn't actually sleeping. He was tied to the master bed, not able to wander around and interrupt her thinking with his constant whining and his puppy dog eyes.

Should she do this?

She was done with Grant. When he came back from China she would tell him so. Or, she would just empty his bank accounts, sell what she could, and be gone when he returned.

Returned to his son who was now a girl.

But should she do that?

On one hand, Lucas wanted to be feminized. He dreamed of it. It was in his eyes and his swishing walk.

If she wanted to be mean to him, she wouldn't go through with it. She would leave him a male, and that would make him suffer.

But she didn't have anything against him. In fact, his submission had given her a sense of freedom she had only dreamed about.

So that left Grant, and she was pretty sure he would be upset if he came home and discovered that she had feminized his son.

Of course, technically, it was Lucas's choice. But Grant wouldn't believe that.

Men never believed what was in front of their own faces.

So, there it was. She could please Lucas, who wasn't a bad kid, and really mess with Grant, who wasn't a bad sort, but he was not submissive, treated her like an equal, and not a superior, and…she would do it.

The decision made, she went upstairs to untie Lucas, and maybe give him a quick poke before bed.

Funny how she was obsessed with pile driving his rump. No physical pleasure, but, man, the sense of power!

Incredible.

She entered the bedroom and Lucas raised his head and stared at her. He wasn't a dumb kid, but getting reamed out so often, being made to submit so much, he was developing a serious drool for her. All he wanted to do was follow her around and beg.

He had no hope of getting out of his chastity tube, but he still begged, as if he had hope.

Silly boy.

She walked to the bed and gazed down at him.

"Mmmphppjo!"

She had put a penis gag in his mouth and yet he tried to speak to her.

The lad never learned.

She sat on the edge of the bed and played with his chastity tube. He had a nice big cock in there. Well, big when it wasn't forced to be small.

She slapped his balls and smiled as he jerked.

He wasn't naked. He wore a bra with the cups ripped out, sissy panties, and his hair was long and styled and his lips were plumped and painted.

"Settle down, sweetheart," she spoke soothingly.

Still he tried to talk, so she put a finger into his backside.

"If you don't settle down I'll take this out."

He was caught now, and he shut up and wiggled his butt, begged for more silently, his desperate, brown eyes doing the talking.

"Now, Lucas, I have decided that we must move you along."

He wrinkled his eyebrows in question.

"Tomorrow I'll arrange for you to get some boobs. Some big ones.

Would you like that? Nod if you do."

He nodded, and his eyes looked so happy.

"Furthermore, I'll try to get you some liposuction, move that baby fat of yours where it will do some real good."

He wasn't sure what that meant, but he looked so excited.

"The thing I wanted to ask you, would you like to get HRT? Hormone Replacement Therapy?"

He frowned, so she explained.

We can get you estrogen, and that will give you a more feminine shape. your boobs might get even bigger."

He smiled around the penis gag.

"And we can get you testosterone blocker. That will make your dick shrink. If you don't want a big dick, then you need the blockers. But if you want to retain your wonderful penis size, even though you can't use it while in chastity, then you shouldn't take the testosterone blockers.

She reached up to where his hand was fastened to the bed post. "Squeeze once for yes, two for no. Do you want the estrogen?"

One squeeze.

"And how about the testosterone? Do you want a small dick? If you do, then squeeze once."

He squeezed twice.

"Oh, too bad. I'd really like to see you with a cute little button of a peeny. But that's okay. As long as we keep you locked up it'll be okay. So yes to estrogen, no to testosterone blockers. Is that right?"

He nodded, then remembered to squeeze once.

"Excellent. Now, it is that time of night." Which was a funny statement, because what she did next did not require day or night for her to do it.

She reached into the toy drawer, the lowest drawer in her night stand, and took out a small whip. It was only a foot long, and it wasn't made of stiff strands or any hard objects.

She climbed up on the bed and mounted his face and faced his feet.

"MPHHHFHHT!"

"Don't worry, I'll let you breath. Just be careful with your teeth. I don't want you to break them on my rings."

Shiela had four rings in each labium, eight total. They were big and thick and they jangled when she walked, or when she was active down there.

Lucas kept his lips over his teeth.

Shiela pulled her rings apart until it looked like she had flaps for labia. She lowered her pure pinkness onto his face.

"Oh, yes," she groaned as she ground her hole down on his nose, then she started slapping his balls with the little whip.

Lucas shrieked, but the sound was muffled by her 'flaps.

But the shrieks caused a unique vibration in her pussy. She felt the sensations rocket through her.

"Oh, yeah," she moaned, and she kept slapping him.

The soft strands struck his balls and each strike made him jerk, made him jam his face upward into her heavenly slit.

Every fourth or fifth stroke she lifted up enough so he could gasp a time or two, then she lowered herself again.

Smack. Smack. Smack.

His head jerking upward, his tongue lapping the length of her slit, and it wasn't long before Shiela was arching her back and rolling her eyeballs back in her skull.

She slumped forward, allowing him to breath, then she weakly crawled off him.

Lucas was sobbing. His face was a puffy mess of pussy juices, and his make up was a mess.

Now tired, Shiela loosened his wrists and ankles and said, "Go to bed. Don't talk. Shoo."

He crawled off the bed. He was so beaten he crawled across the floor, couldn't make it to his feet until he was halfway down the hall.

Shiela slid under the sheets and closed her eyes. She went to sleep with a smile on her face.

The next morning Shiela arose early. She was cheerful and couldn't wait to get started. She strode down the hall in her negligee, her proud bust leading the way, her round rump swaying sexily behind her.

She walked into Lucas's room and pulled the blankets off him.

"What…what?"

He looked tired. Probably didn't get much sleep the night previous. After all, his squirming dick, fighting the cock cage like a man in a flea barrel, he probably didn't get to sleep until near dawn.

That was okay. She could just cover the rings around his eyes with make up.

"Get up. Fix breakfast. Eggs Benedict and…do you know how to fix Eggs Benedict?"

He shook his head, and she almost laughed. The circles around his eyes made him look like a raccoon, and the motion of his head was quick like a hamster.

"Well, crap. Okay. Over hard. Sausage, you probably don't know the right way to cook bacon. And French toast. You can do that, can't you?"

He nodded. It looked like he was afraid to talk. He certainly wasn't afraid to follow her with his soft brown eyes.

"I'm going to make some phone calls, and we'll fix you up after breakfast."

That brightened him up.

Shiela headed for the living room. She picked up her cell phone and headed out to the book. As she walked she dialed.

"I'm looking for somebody to perform some plastic surgery. I need vacation boobs…no. Make that full implants. Big ones. And I need some liposuction. You don't? Then who should I call?"

It took her a half dozen calls, and she was going to be charged four times the asking price, but that was okay. Grant had plenty of money.

She laughed. When he found out that he had paid for his own son's feminization…ha!

Lucas served her breakfast. Good boy. He didn't call her, just took it on himself to bring out her eggs and sausage and French toast to the pool area.

"Go eat," she said, "but only half portions. You will be getting an operation this afternoon."

"You mean it?" he asked eagerly, unable to stop himself.

She smiled. It was exciting. "Yes. You'll get your boobs. Oh, and I'd like some apple juice."

He nearly skipped when he left the patio.

After breakfast she sat him down and began preparing his face.

"This is cleanser…for the pores." She showed him the small sponge that had turned black in removing the dirt from his pores.

"All that?"

"Yep. Now this is primer. We're going to remove imperfections, and make a canvas for your make up."

Foundation and blush, she continued working on him. She used brushes that felt so light and downright ticklish on his face.

She spent some time on his eyes, making them look dusty and sexy and mysterious. Then she plumped his lips again, she wanted him to look like Angeline Jolie, and painted them red.

As she studied him, and he studied himself in the mirror, she wondered out loud. "We should probably look into permanent make up for you."

He looked unsure about that, but it didn't matter. She'd make up his mind for him.

Finally, she brushed his hair and she got out her ear piercing kit. She put a couple of quick holes in his lobes and dangled a pair of dangly earrings from his ears.

He studied the earrings carefully, and he was trying to withhold a smile.

"We're going to pierce your nipples eventually, a couple of weeks maybe," she told him.

He looked at her and seemed okay with that. Not that it mattered.

"We might even pierce your cock. It would be nice to pierce it, get rid of the chastity tube, and just tie it to your thigh, or pull it back towards your crack."

He frowned, and he seemed to be in thought, but, again, it didn't matter. She was in charge here.

"Okay, let's get you dressed. Since you're probably going to have to disrobe for the operation, let's just put you in panties, skirt and blouse. No bra."

She handed him a blouse. It was sheer and transparent.

"But somebody might see my nipples?" he complained.

"Good," she answered. "Are you good with tools?"

"I'm okay," he hesitated, wondering what she was going to say next.

He had his panties and skirt on, and as he slipped into the blouse and looked down at his nipples in dismay she said, "I'm going to need you to remodel the basement.

She got out her finger nail kit and began sizing fakes on his nails.

"Your father and I discussed it before he left, and he agreed that I needed a dungeon to take care of you."

"To me? You talked to my father about…about…"

"Yup. He knows I'm feminizing you," she lied. "He knows about all the other stuff, the boobs and the piercings, everything."

That caused Lucas to be very, very silent as he thought about that. That was beyond embarrassing, it was beyond dressing up, or even getting operations.

This was his whole self image being discarded.

But, whatever it was, it didn't seem of concern to Shiela. She was gluing fakes on his nails, and they were much longer than he expected.

Not that he really knew what he expected.

They were a half inch longer than his own nails, and they changed his nails from slightly spatulate to pretty ovals. She began painting them a metallic red. Very shiny. Then gloss and fixer.

These nails were here to stay!

"So when we're done today I'm going to want you to start cleaning out the dungeon. The basement. I want everything moved into the garage. Make a pile for stuff to be discarded, and a pile for stuff we can sell. Then I'm going to want you to wash everything, scrub the walls, and when they're dry, to paint them. I want them black, and I want you to drill some holes and put in some eye screws.

He stared at his hands as she continued explaining what she wanted. He was stunned by how sexy his hands were. They looked longer, which made them look more slender.

He looked in the mirror and held them up to his face.

Shiela had shadowed his face and covered up male characteristics, and emphasized female characteristics.

He really did look female. He was probably 25% female before this all started. Now he was over fifty per cent. A quick glance and people would think of him as female. A longer glance might enable them to see the maleness underneath.

But…damn. He felt good. And his weenie really felt good. It had been wiggling in the tube all morning, pushing hard sometimes, moving around sometimes as if it was looking for a better position to try and break out.

"Did you hear me?" asked Shiela.

"I think so."

"What do I want?"

"You want me to clean the basement, wash it, paint it, put eye screws in the walls and get some chains and stuff."

"Very good. And I want it done by this weekend."

He nodded. Darn. That was a lot of work, but he figured he could get it done.

Heck, he had to get it done. He wanted Shiela to spank him some more. And he wanted to be drained, and maybe she'd even chain him to the basement wall and do things to him.

He smiled at Shiela, totally enthralled, totally submitted and wanting nothing more than to submit further.

She leaned forward and patted his cheek, then she carefully touched her lips to his.

He near swooned.

Grant's money working. Shiela walked Lucas into a clinic at two in the afternoon.

The most difficult thing was the paperwork. There were questions for trans people, how long they had wanted to change their sex, that sort of thing, but in the end they proved inconsequential. While the receptionist was trying to get answers, and Shiela was lying her face off, a nurse came out and called them. Paperwork incomplete, Shiela smiled victoriously as she and Lucas walked back into the clinic.

They were shown to a small operating theater. Lucas undressed and was placed on a table. A young, Japanese man smiled at him, chatted for a brief moment, then put the gas mask over his face.

Shiela sat in a corner and watched quietly. She wanted to see this, and she was afraid the doctor might kick her out.

She didn't have to worry, the doctor was a little high, and she wanted to talk about this and that and everything.

She was actually a striking woman underneath her scrubs, with large breasts, which turned out to be implants. The doctor obviously ate her own cooking.

Shiela watched as the operation commenced.

First, the doctor placed plastic bags on Lucas's chest and looked to Shiela for the correct size.

Shiela picked the largest ones, and the doctor agreed.

"Would you like me to make his nipples stick up?"

"Could you?"

"No problemo."

The doctor injected silicone under the nipples and they poked out like Lucas was awake and excited.

The doctor made incisions below the pectorals then slid the bags under his nipples. He had instant boobs and Shiela was amazed. They looked so perfectly lifelike.

"I notice he's got a chastity tube. There are other methods, you know."

"Really?" Shiela tilted her head in curiosity.

"Oh, yes. We can give him a shot of depo provera, then sew his penis back between his legs. I mention this because we were talking about hormones, and..." she shrugged as she glued the slits beneath Lucas's boobs closed.

"Will those boobs sag?"

"No. I hooked them onto his rib cage. He'll be stand up pretty. Or maybe I should say 'she'll' be stand up pretty.

"What would you do with his balls if we went ahead with the depo?"

"We push them back into the little canal they descended from. Quite easy, quite safe. The bonus is that his libido will be relatively unaffected. He'll be horny, but unable to do anything about it. And as time goes on he'll get nothing but more horny."

"Well, let me think about it, I'll discuss it with him, and get back to you."

"Excellent. Now, let's discuss the liposuction." Suddenly she paused and looked around. "What's that jangling sound."

Shiela pursed her lips and hid a smile. But as the doctor kept looking up and around, she decided she better come clean. She didn't want the doctor distracted while she worked on Lucas.

"I've got piercings."

"Piercings?" The doctor lowered her gaze to Shiela's chest, but saw no sign of jewelry. She looked lower. "Down there?"

"I've got four thick rings on each labium."

"Can I see?"

Shiela looked at Lucas, but Lucas was asleep. She looked at the Japanese anesthesiologist.

"Don't worry about Hitaki. He's gay."

Shiela shrugged and lifted her dress and lowered her panties.

"Oh, Lord, those are beautiful!"

The eight rings pulled Shiela's labia down a little, and she gave a wiggle of her hips and made them sing.

"That's incredible! I'm going to have to get some." Then she frowned. "But how do you stop them from jangling.

"If I was really wanting them to be quiet I just tie them together. The extra bonus is that if I want to go out, but don't feel like putting out, with men, I mean, I just put a padlock through them. That tends to keep them quiet, too. But I like it when they sing."

"When they sing," chuckled the doctor delightedly. "Do you mind? Can you slide up on the table so I can really examine them?"

"Sure." Shiela stepped on a slide out platform on another table, then sat on the corner, her legs dangling to the sides.

The doctor moved in and eyed the rings, and her pussy, from about eight inches away.

"May I feel them?"

"Knock yourself out," Shiela said with a grin.

The doctor gingerly touched the rings. She felt them, lifted them, and even tugged very gently. "That doesn't hurt."

"Oh, no." Pull on them slowly. Everything stretches."

The doctor pulled, and pulled. The labia pulled out.

The doctor pulled them apart and Shiela gave a slight moan as her pinkness was totally on display.

"Do these enhance sexual feeling?"

"Oh, you better believe it. Touch me."

The doctor was wearing latex gloves and she poked a finger between the spread out labia. She pressed the pad of her index finger to the pink and Shiela twitched and gave a louder moan.

"Unless you've got a dick, you'd better stop."

The doc laughed and removed her hand, let go of the rings.

The rings jangled as Shiela slipped off the table and onto the floor.

"Well, you've certainly inspired me, but I suppose we better get back to the matter at hand."

The matter at hand was liposuction, and after a short discussion the doctor turned on the machine, and it sounded exactly like a vacuum cleaner.

Lucas had some love handles. He was slender, but under the normal clothes he wore were little rolls of fat.

The doctor sucked out that fat and deposited it into his hips. In a short time Lucas had round hips, just like a girl's.

"Well, that's about it," the doctor shut the machine off and examined Lucas's face. "It's a pity. I could move the fat in his face, redistribute it, but the work is too fine. I don't want him to have a bumpy face. His face is so soft and pretty…"

"What do you suggest?"

"Hormone Replacement Therapy."

"We discussed that."

"Yes. I've prepared a prescription for you, but I would ask that you reconsider the testosterone blockers."

"Why's that?"

"Many trans people would like the smallest dick possible. I understand why you might want him to retain his size, he's quite sexy, and it's fun to use those big honker dicks, but there are always vibrators. Besides, if his penis is shrunken by hormones and then I sew it up, he'll have a perfectly female mound down there."

Shiela nodded. "I have a feeling we'll be calling you shortly. But for right now…"

"I'll tell you what, I'll include a prescription for testosterone blockers, and you can use it if you wish. Also, I'll include pills to make his cock go limp quickly. just a few days. They'll last a year, so use them at your discretion."

"That is wonderful! Thank you so much!"

"Anything for the sisterhood. Now then, I'm done. Would you like me to wake him up?"

"Of course."

The doctor nodded to the gas man and he turned a stopcock and the whistling sound of gas through tubes died down. Within thirty seconds Lucas's eyes were fluttering.

"Pleasure doing business with you," said the doctor, squeezing Shiela's forearm, let me know." Then she was gone.

The gas man busied himself with the machine, and Lucas tried to sit up.

"Wow. I feel like I was just on a bender, but no real headache."

Then he looked down at his chest.

It was enormous, and his nipples were like little spikes.

"Oh, my God!" he whispered. His tones were most reverent.

"They really are quite beautiful, aren't they," murmured Shiela, cupping his new tits with her hands and hefting them.

Lucas, like any girl, shivered and drew away.

"Stop that," said Shiela.

He overcame his reluctance to be felt up and moved forward.

Shiela lifted his tits. She palpated them softly. She touched his nipples and he gave a real shiver then, but not of fright, of pleasure.

"Oh, that feels good."

The pleasure in his nipples radiated out through his boobs, into his chest. His penis started struggling in its cage.

He looked down at his groin. "Was I trying to get erect while I was under?"

"I didn't notice."

"You did," mentioned the anesthesiologist, turning off the gas canister and standing up. "I was watching."

Then he left the room.

Shiela and Lucas were alone, Shiela's hands still fondling his breasts, grinning as he tried hopelessly to get stiff.

"Well, let's go home. I want to play with you this afternoon."

With that they headed out.

It was four o'clock when they arrived home, and Lucas was quite awake, and quite excited.

He ran into the bedroom and quickly put on a bra. "Ah," he sighed in relief. "They're heavy."

Shiela had followed him, and she laughed as he sighed and turned in front of the mirror.

His body, except for the chastity cage, was perfect. His butt poked out just enough and was perfectly round.

His tits were supported by the hooks on the implants, but Lucas wanted to wear a bra.

He wanted to experience everything feminine.

He put on a garter and nylons.

He selected a dress out of Shiela's closet.

He stepped into his high heels.

It felt wonderful. To have real tits, to perfectly represent the female form, it was more than he had ever dreamed of.

Shiela then sat him down and began making him over.

He had worn the bare necessities to the doctor's office, but now Shiela laid it on. She took her time and transformed his face.

He was totally female on the body, but his face still had masculine characteristics.

Of course he had a soft face, oval with petulant lips, but the make up was doing the job. When Shiela was done he was 90% female. More than enough to fool any man.

Then Shiela sat him on the bed and sat down next to him, facing him.

"Lucas, it's time we had a serious discussion."

"Oh?" He looked a little worried at how serious Shiela had become.

"Yes. Now, you've got a penis, and it's a good one, but do you really need it?

"What do you mean?"

"The doctor gave me two extra prescriptions. One will block testosterone, and that should shrink your penis. The other will make you limp."

"No more hard ons?"

"Do you need them? After all, it appears that you like anal sex better."

"But what if I don't like it?"

"Then we stop the pills and you return to normal."

"My dick will get big again?"

"Of course." Shiela didn't have the faintest idea, but she didn't care. Besides, she had a feeling he wasn't going to be wanting his dick to be big again.

"Well, I don't know."

Shiela did know. Grant would eventually be coming back, and she wanted to have Lucas as complete as possible in his transformation.

"Look, Lucas, the world was not won by people who hesitated. If you like what is happening, then we should just go for it."

"Well, I…uh…"

"Come on, out with it. What's really bothering you?"

"Well, uh…"

"What?"

"I'm a virgin."

Shiela blinked and sat back.

He was 19 years old and a virgin? In this day and age?

"I just never figured out how to talk to girls, and Ive…you've noticed I had an attitude.

'Had' and attitude. He certainly didn't now.

"So that's all that's bothering you."

"Yes." He was looking down, his long hair covering his face, totally embarrassed.

"Okay, I've got a deal for you."

He looked up and brushed his hair back.

God, she loved how soft and sparkly his brown eyes were.

"It takes a while for pills to work. I give you the pills and you get to fuck me. As much as you want, until the pills take effect."

"Really?"

"Remember, we don't know how long, you might get soft in an hour, it might take a week, but until your dick is no longer hard, you can fuck the shit out of me."

Lucas was all grins. "All right!"

Oddly, Shiela was looking forward to this. She could feel her pussy pulse at the idea of being his first, last and only fuck. Talk about power!

She stood up and went to the bag filled with prescription medicine. "Come on. Let's have you take your pills on a full stomach.

They went to the kitchen and Shiela fixed BLT sandwiches. She watched as Lucas ate the sandwiches and sipped on a Coke. She even added a dollop of whiskey to the Coke. She wanted to make this as easy as possible.

"There goes the estrogen," he smiled as he downed a few small, pink pills.

He sipped, swished, and swallowed. The pills rolled down his tube to stomachland.

"Here are the testosterone blockers."

"These don't make me limp, but I'll get softer, and smaller, over time."

"You got it."

He looked at the three blue pills in his hand. They were a little bigger than the estrogen pills.

He tossed them down his throat and sipped more Coke. He blinked, and the enormity of what he had just done settled over him. Changing more completely into a woman. His penis getting smaller and smaller. Eventually it would be about as big as a five year old's.

But there was one last pill.

Shiela moved over next to him, her breasts touched him. She cupped one of his breasts. "This is crazy, but let me feed you this last pill."

"This is it," he said, staring at the lone pill in his hand.

"This is it. It's a year of no boners."

"God, I hope…"

"You hope what?"

"Well, I hope I like sex with my dick, but if I like it too much then…then I've made a mistake. But I'll be stuck with it for a year.

"Honey, from my experience men always like anal sex better. I don't think you have anything to worry about."

He nodded. "Okay."

She put her hand to his mouth. He opened his mouth and she popped the pill in. He gulped without Coke.

He looked scared, and excited at the same time. His stomach was tying itself in knots.

What had he done.

She held his face, gently, and softly kissed him. It was long and passionate, then she moved away from him.

"Should we take off my chastity tube?" he asked.

"What? What for?"

"So I can fuck you."

"Sure you can fuck me, but I didn't say anything about taking off your tube."

"But…but…how am I supposed to…"

She shrugged, her mouth a huge smile, laughter bubbling up out of her. "I have no idea.

Then she was laughing hysterically, and Lucas felt like crying.

Part Two

Lucas stared down at his poor penis. It was never going to get to fuck anybody! He was going to die a virgin! Locked away in its own, little prison cell.

Tears dropped from his eyes onto his boobs. It was never even going to get hard again. When she finally did let him out of the chastity cage, if she did, his penis would be limp, shrinking.

Sniffling, he looked up at Shiela.

She was grinning. An ear to ear show of happy teeth.

"How could you do this to me?"

She said, "Just kidding." And started laughing again. Hilariously. "Oh, the look on your face! Like you just lost your best friend!"

She patted his cheek and quipped, "Of course you did, didn't you."

"Then you're not going to…"

"Well, I should. It's all you deserve, a lifetime of frustration, but…" she produced the key and said, "Come to me."

He stood and moved towards her, his hips thrust forward, looking over his big knockers and holding his chastity cage in one hand.

She gripped the prison and slipped the key into the lock. A quick twist—click—and the thing fell off him.

Now he sobbed in gratitude.

His penis immediately sprouted. He hadn't been in chastity long, but a little time is a long time when you're confined like that.

"Oh, yes," she murmured, watching appreciatively as his dingus swelled up and poked forth.

He cried more, and she grabbed his dick in her hand and began to stroke it.

Immediately he was ready to cum.

She laughed and let go. "Take it easy, tiger. You want to get in me, don't you?"

He nodded, his tears spattering his boobs and hers.

"Then come on." She grabbed him by the tool and pulled him out of the kitchen.

They walked through the foyer and up the stairs, then down the long hall.

"Oh…oh…you better hurry."

"NO hurry," she said, squeezing his cock. She turned and pulled him to her. She gripped his mouth with her lips and began working it.

He was in heaven, feeling the thrill of his cock, the sensations shooting out from her hand. His balls felt like they were going to explode.

Then she broke the kiss and continued dragging him towards the bedroom.

She entered the bedroom and pulled him around, put her hand on his chest, above his boobs, and pushed.

He fell back on the bed, his boobs juddered, and he stared at her.

God, she was beautiful.

She slipped out of her clothes quickly, watching him, gauging him.

His cock pointed towards her, and he slowly unbuttoned his blouse and shed it.

His bra held him, but just barely. the bulge of flesh overflowed the brassiere, and he knew he was going to have get a bigger one. And even bigger ones once the hormone treatments started working.

She moved towards him and said, "I'm going to make your first fuck a memorable one."

"You don't have to worry about that," he was almost drooling as he eyed her marvelous mounds.

She turned him over and slapped his ass. "All fours, bitch."

"What? But I thought I was going to fuck you! We've. already done this!"

"Trust me, Lucas. This is the way it's got to be."

While he watched over his shoulder, from the doggy position, she opened the drawer of her little side table and took out a strap on.

She loved screwing like a man more than anything. She felt nothing physically, but the sense of power that swallowed her up was like Columbus discovering the new world.

She fastened the straps and screwed in a large dildo. Real large, because Lucas was ready.

She stepped forward and greased him. She used lots of lube and reamed him and opened him up and got him ready, then she went to town.

Lucas gave way under her weight, then he arched his back and pushed his butt towards her.

She was all the way in, firmly seated, and she began twisting and corkscrewing.

Lucas was near out of his mind with the golden glow that was emanating from his rectum. He felt so full, so happy, and it wasn't long before he began draining.

Shiela measured him carefully. This was the hard part. If she drained him too much he might be soft. Many men wouldn't be, but this was unique to Lucas.

But if she didn't drain him enough he would cum.

Yes, she wanted him to cum, but not too soon.

And she didn't want him cumming hard. She wanted to do something with his orgasm.

For long minutes she screwed him. He was crying out in ecstasy, pushing back furiously, winding his cheeks up and pressing back on her plastic thingie.

Then she simply pulled out of him.

"Hey!"

"Be patient, little one," she smiled as she took off the strap on. Then she climbed onto the bed, turned over and spread her legs.

She had drained him just enough. He was harder than a nail and ready to go. But he was empty.

Now, instead of pushing back, he was pushing forward.

He ground into her, desperate for a squirt, and she lay back and enjoyed the ride.

The minutes passed and she let him drill her mercilessly.

She had orgasms. Sequential, one after another, and she just folded her arms behind her head and grunted and sighed.

He ravished her tits, sucking on the nipples, squeezing them, pummeling them.

She had more orgasms, and it was building. She was now breathless. She had screwed like this before, but not often. It was too easy to lose her mind and go crazy.

She didn't want to go crazy, she wanted him to go crazy.

Minutes passed, he pumped and humped, but the big O eluded him. Then, exhausted, he slowed down.

"I can't do it."

"Oh, you'll get there."

He rested.

She gave him good liquor and played with his boobs while she waited.

He tried again. And tried and tried and tried.

He was getting closer, but here was the nefarious part of Shiela's plan.

He was near empty of semen. He couldn't cum until he built more up. And, finally, enough semen built so he could have an orgasm.

But he only had a little semen, so he only had a little orgasm.

He cried and felt a pathetic, little squirt come out of him.

Where was the eyeball rolling, toe curling orgasm he had heard about? Where was the earth shattering crack of thunder? The gates of heaven opening to the golden glow of spiritual and physical golden lava?

He simply didn't have enough sperm for that. He hadn't had enough recovery time, and so the big orgasm he had waited for, worked for, was nothing but a spit and dull frustration.

He lay there, a little bit of semen leaking out of his cock, gasping.

"Is that it? Is that the big orgasm people talk about?"

"Of course it is, honey." She was again on her side, touching his nipples, playing with his boobs, and watching him.

"But it was so…so…small."

"Not like when you take it up the ass."

"No," he admitted.

"When you orgasm the girl way the world stops. Even if you don't orgasm, you get the golden glow of satisfaction, and it just permeates your body and soul and leaves you amazed."

He nodded, biting his lip, thoroughly disappointed.

"Well, don't worry. We'll probably have a few days to try again."

But Lucas didn't really care. Heck, if it was up to him, twenty/twenty hindsight, he would have remained a virgin. It was that disappointing.

As for Shiela, she smiled, and exulted on the inside. She didn't want him getting all enthused about cocking a girl. She wanted him craving the female way of doing things. So she had deliberately drained him, made him work too hard, and done all she could to make sure he had the worst and most lacking orgasm in the history of fucking.

And she had succeeded.

She took him to the basement.

The basement was accessible from the garage. A door in the corner of the garage that led down under the house.

It was a big basement. The house was over 3,000 feet, and the basement ran the length and half the width, for about 1500 square feet.

They reached the bottom of the stairs and looked down the dark distance.

The walls were cement, but they were so dirty they might have been painted black. There were a few cobwebs, but these were old and slowly disintegrating.

There were three windows alongside the high ceiling. They were a foot and a half long and maybe eight inches tall. They let in light, but nobody was going to be crawling through them.

There were three lights in line, and they were dim bulbs indeed. They cast an orangish glow that made everything look dull and gloomy.

At the far end was a small room that looked like it might have held coal at one time. Though why a modern house would need coal was something that required a bit of thought.

There was debris in the basement, but not much. A few boxes. A table. Bits of rubbish littering the long floor.

There were two drains, but no evidence that any water had ever gone down them.

It was dirty and sterile at the same time.

The two women—Lucas was considering himself such now—stared at the grim scene.

"I want everything cleaned up. The walls scrubbed with soap, then everything painted black. And I want it done fast."

She was thinking that several days had passed, and she wanted to be done with everything long before Grant came home.

"Okay."

Lucas was fully made up. Wearing a beautiful dress of silk and a ring of pearls around his neck. He had earrings that glittered in the light, and his hair was done up in the French style.

"I should go get changed."

"No."

"But I might make a mess of my pretty clothes!"

"This is an exercise in how to stay feminine. No matter if you have to lift heavy, or use a paint brush, you have to do it as a woman. No backing out now."

Lucas understood what she meant. She had spoken to him long the night before, while she pounded his ass, about the need for a woman to stay beautiful. And now he had to.

"So, get to work, and I'll make a couple of drinks."

Shiela sashayed up the steps, her heels clicking even on those treads.

Lucas stared at the filth and debris, and dreaded it. He was pretty now, and he didn't want to make a mess of himself.

Still, he had to do what he had to do.

He walked over to a box and picked it up. He tried to hold it away from his body, but dust got on his breasts, made circles on his dress right on the boobs.

Sighing, trying to hold it away from himself, he walked up the steps and made his way to the garage.

While Lucas emptied the basement and prepared it for washing, Shiela made a couple of zombie cocktails. She had a feeling Lucas was going to need a stiff drink, and there was nothing stiffer than a zombie, if you can forgive the pun.

She put in three types of rum, then lime, grapefruit, bitters, Pernod and grenadine.

She took a sip to make sure it was passable.

It was sweet, a bit fruity, and had the kick of a mule on steroids.

She smacked her lips and headed for the basement.

Lucas was pushing a broom, maneuvering a pile of dust and splinters and whatnot down the length of the basement. He had the two round spots on his tits, there were streaks of dust on his forehead, and his hair was coming loose.

"Here go," Shiela handed him a drink.

Lucas sipped, and appreciated the way the cold concoction slid down his throat and exploded in his belly.

"Whoo," he said. "I needed that."

"You need something else, too," said Shiela, looking down at his crotch.

Upstairs they went, and an hour later Lucas came down, limp, but disappointed. God, for so much work one would think there would be a heaven sized bang. But...orgasms just were too much work and not a lot of fun.

Upstairs, laying on her back with her legs spread, her pussy ravished, and a thin trickle of weak semen leaking out of her slit, Shiela smiled.

Everything was perfect. She was getting a ton of orgasms, and poor Lucas was getting nothing but a thin squirt and frustration.

And when he was done he talked about how much better anal orgasms were.

But she was tired, and he had work to do, and she wanted him even more frustrated. So she stalled him, promised to do him that night.

She wanted to give him a chance to build up so she could drain him and make him even less able.

And she wondered when the testosterone blockers would work.

She was looking forward to the estrogen, of course, but he was already female looking. She wanted his weenie to shrink.

Downstairs Lucas finished sweeping. Went outside for the garden hose, hooked it up to the slop sink in the laundry room, and began washing the walls.

He was a mess. He had dust on him that, in the now humid basement, was turning into mud.

His hair was a mess because he had to brush it to keep it out of his eyes, and his hands were wet and dirty.

His make up was disintegrating as he was sweating copiously.

He thought about being a woman, and the fact that woman should never do such jobs. Leave that stuff for the men. Let the men get filthy, dirty and sweaty.

And he dreamed of Shiela taking him. Of being bent over and fill ed with her latex cock, or by one of her vibrators or dildos or whatever.

He didn't miss being a man at all.

A week later two things happened.

First, the basement was painted and dried and ready for the 'jewelry.'

Second, his penis was waning. And thank God!

He was tired of screwing and getting so little return for his effort.

Of course he was glad Shiela had gotten so much pleasure. She was so nice to him, and he lived for her groans when she came.

But as for himself, he just wanted to be bent over the bed, or the couch, or the table, and feel Shiela move into him.

She had taken him in every room, and that had been exciting.

Sometimes it was difficult, his thighs made sore by table edges. Sometimes it was wonderful, all fours with his shoulders slumped down and her using the big dildo.

And all the time it was better than dick sex.

"Okay, honey, whatcha got for me?"

They walked around the basement, their heels clicking loudly.

Lucas was actually looking pretty good. As he got more used to wearing female clothes he managed to stay cleaner.

Oh, he needed work, but…he was learning.

And he was learning how to walk. His heels were starting to make that powerful click, click, click sound.

"How do you want the eye screws?"

"Oh, I would say stagger them. One here, then six feet further on another one, then a foot, then six feet, spaced all the way down the basement.

Lucas did the mental math. The basement was 50 feet long. 6 times 8 was 48.

"I can probably fit 7 people in. 8 if you want to crunch it."

"7 would be good. While you're doing that I'm going to order some special furniture."

Lucas began drilling holes in the masonry. It took special drill bits and water to keep the bits cool, but it wasn't all that difficult. When he had all the holes drilled he screwed the eye screws in. they were big and would hold sturdy lengths of chains.

He knew it would be chains because she had bought a couple of rolls of chain and it was upstairs, in the garage.

What he didn't understand was the 'furniture.'

Some of it was in crates, and she had him open them so she could inspect the shipments. Padded planks, specially carved, that didn't look like any furniture he had ever seen.

Some double thick planks. Some leather restraints, pieces of weird hardware.

But Lucas was too busy mounting the screws to bother with that stuff. He would find out when it was time.

When he was done with the screws it was time.

He broke open a crate and assembled the contents.

It was a rack. A real rack, with ropes that could be pulled tight, and a bed of planks, and straps for the ankles and wrists.

Lucas stared at Shiela. "Where did you get this?"

"I had it specially made. How do you like it?"

"It's...scary."

Shiela just smiled happily.

Another crate held a spanking bench. It was complete with padded area for the body and a machine that spun eight big paddles.

"What is this for?" Now he was really feeling nervous.

"I want to go into politics."

He blinked, but kept assembling the contraptions.

A chair with nubs on the seat. The nubs weren't super sharp, but they were VERY uncomfortable. And the two front legs were shorter than the back legs, which meant that anybody sitting in the chair would automatically slide forward. It would be a constant effort to not rub the butt raw.

A 'Judas Cradle.' That was a pyramid thing with a pointy top. Shiela had Lucas arrange ropes to hold a person atop the thing, on their anus. Ouch.

And there were other things. Some small, like a scold's bridle, or a pear of anguish, some large, like a St. Andrew's Cross.

And there were boxes and boxes of things like whips, paddles, chastity tubes, anal invaders, and so on and so on and so on.

A month passed.

Lucas was exhausted. Now that he was no longer trying to fuck with his dick, he was taking it up the butt, but Shiela was screwing him less and less, letting his juices build. He was so excited all the time that he couldn't sleep. So he worked.

Shiela would be sleeping away upstairs and he would be pounding, sawing, screwing and trying to keep his female clothes clean and his make up from wearing off.

And the hormones were starting to really take effect.

His penis looked smaller, and it hung so limp. His breasts were getting slightly bigger. His face was shifting as the fat was redistributed. His cheeks changed, his eyes looked bigger and more scintillating.

And he liked it.

He loved to just stand in front of mirror and look at himself. As a man he had been lacking, weak, wimpy. As a woman he was robust, sexy, happy.

But for all this, the basement was finished.

Shiela woke up and was pleased to find Lucas waiting for her. He was cleaned up, make up hid the circles around his eyes, and he said, "It's done."

Shiela took a tour, and she liked what she saw. Everything was to her specifications. The furniture was perfectly assembled. The ambience of the basement was absolutely cool.

She turned to Lucas. "Let's try it out!"

She was excited, her eyes aglow, and her breathing was labored.

This was the moment Lucas was worried about. He knew she was going to have him on the furniture, and…he didn't want to be tortured.

But she wasn't thinking of pain. Well, not just pain.

Rather, a mix of pain and pleasure that was beyond exciting.

Lucas sat down on the padded planks that were the bed and turned longways.

Shiela fastened straps to his ankles and to his wrists, and proceeded to turn the wheel.

He began to groan as his joints stretched. It was getting uncomfortable, but not yet painful, when she suddenly stopped.

"What are you doing?" he asked, gasping for breath.

"Experimenting," she answered, and she picked up a whip with broad strips.

SMACK! He cried out, but…it was only a little pain. Not enough to do more than scare him.

She delivered a half a dozen strokes, frowned, then traded the whip for a paddle.

But the paddle didn't please her either.

"This is all wrong," she murmured. "Turn over." She began loosening the ropes so he could.

"What?" he protested as the ropes grew slack. He had enough slack to turn over, but he didn't want.

"Turn over. We're done with this side. It doesn't work."

"I'm not going to turn over!"

She laughed. "Lucas, if you don't turn over I'll never fuck your ass again."

That was more of an argument than Lucas could fight. Grunting, unhappy, he turned. The ropes were crossed at his feet and his hands, but Shiela loosened his restraints one at a time and straightened everything out.

Now Lucas was face down, which didn't matter to his little, limp cock.

And there was the realization that she now had access to his happy hole.

Shiela grabbed the flat stripped whip again and began hitting him. This time she worked up a sweat. She didn't hit hard enough to cut, just made his hide bright red.

Lucas's skin was hot now, and when his flesh was properly burning, Shiela rubbed him with that old concoction of capsaicin from chili peppers, piperine from black pepper, and gingerol, from ginger.

Now his flesh was scorching, but before it reached the point of pain she distracted him. First she used a large boa feather and tickled him. It distracted him, but he wasn't laughing. He did wiggle uncontrollably, however.

Then she used a Wharton wheel. Running the little circular saw hand tool up and down over his spanked area.

That hurt, but it also turned him on.

"How's that?" she kept asking. "What's that feel like?"

He did his best to answer.

She used ice on his burning flesh, used her fingernails to claw him, and tried a dozen different things.

When she was done, and Lucas was sobbing and completely immersed in a contradiction of pain and pleasure, she let him loose.

"Okay. The Wharton wheel is good, the feather is worthless, and the…" she went on and on, dissecting the effects of each tool, listing pros and cons, and making a decision.

"So remember, if you use the whip, use the wheel. If the client is stubborn, strike hard and pull his balls till he screams."

"Client?"

She ignored his blurt and took him to a bench.

The bench had four platforms, each platform had a 'cuff' on it. He placed his forearm in one cuff and she snapped it closed. Then restrained his other three limbs similarly.

He was stuck in the all fours position. His butt in the air. His head resting on a little platform and unable to do anything but look forward.

Shiela put on a strap on and proceeded to try out the bench. She screwed him for a while, asked him questions, then went to another dildo.

"How's that?"

"Am I far enough in?"

"Does this corkscrew motion excite you?"

"Does it help if I twist your balls?"

On and on, trying out every dildo and vibrator and butt plug she had, which was a lot.

This was a piece of furniture that Lucas liked.

Loved.

He was in heaven, and each dildo seemed better than the last. By the end, even though that had not been her purpose, he was thoroughly drained.

"Oh, my God," he whispered, weak in the knees when Shiela let him up.

And that was it for the day.

She helped him up the stairs and put him on one of the lounge chairs out by the pool.

He sat, and his ass felt like it was burning with pleasure. He was gaping, and he knew it, but that was the way he liked it.

Shiela went for drinks.

While Lucas lay outside and tried to recover from the overpowering pleasure he had received, Shiela decided to make a drink called 'Adios Motherfucker.'

She poured in an insane combination of liqueurs. Tequila, vodka, rum and gin. Four hard liqueurs that seemed diametrically opposed, but when blended in the fashion of Adios Motherfucker were amazing. She mixed in curacao, sour mix and a lemon, then gave the whole thing a spritz of soda water.

She took the drink out to the patio and handed Lucas his and sat down next to him.

He was naked, red, sweaty, and happy.

She slipped out of her clothes and sipped her drink.

"Mmm, good."

He agreed by gulping the whole thing down.

She laughed.

He turned to her. "I don't understand."

"And what, my dear, don't you understand."

"Why are you making a dungeon in the basement?"

"Well," she mused as she sipped, "I originally told your father that I would need a dungeon to tame you."

Lucas didn't blink. He had been tamed.

"Then I realized that there was a business opportunity in a dungeon."

"A business opportunity?"

"Absolutely. Do you know how many people would be willing to pay big bucks for an hour or two in a real, live dungeon, attended to by real, live sex goddesses?"

He stared at her.

"I think I'll wear a dominatrix outfit. Always have a whip coiled over my shoulder. Deep red lipstick, hair up in a top ponytail. I'll take customers down there and whip them to a frenzied froth. I'll put doo dads up their heinie, or their pussy, depending, and I'll tease them. I'll hurt them to the edge of pain, and...we're going to be so rich!"

"You say we, but what's my role in this?"

She turned to him, lay on her side with her big breasts hanging sideways on her chest. "Do you know how much more people would pay to be dominated by a real, live trans?"

Lucas's mouth opened. In truth, he had gone through changes, but there was a part of him that had never acknowledged his true status.

Trans. Transgender. A man with tits, or a woman with a dick. Which? He didn't care, and he didn't think people would care either.

"Which leads us to a little problem."

"What's that?"

"We need to sew your penis up."

They had discussed this, and Lucas wasn't quite convinced.

"Why?"

"Honey. You'll be a trans, and you either need a big honking pecker, or you need to hide it. I guarantee, people will be more drawn to you if you have no peeny showing. They will be curious. Some will even want to be like you. And, truth here, some people are scared when they see a dick that is too big. They actually get scared that you'll do something, that…" she chuckled, "…that a woman will force herself upon them and screw them."

Lucas sat back and thought about it.

His peeny was getting smaller. His balls were shrinking. His tits were getting bigger and he was looking more feminine every day. There was no way he could be mistaken for anything other than a woman. So… what did it matter?

He turned back to her, "And if it doesn't work then I can have my dick… what? Turned loose? The sutures cut?"

"Sure. No problem." She smiled, and then she ignored him.

She had teased him with the idea, and she knew he would go for it.

He was just that kind of guy.

Revenge of the Step Mommy!
It starts with feminization
and ends up in a dungeon!

Grace Mansfield

A Note from the Author!

I love my Step-Mommy.

Unfortunately, I don't have one.

But if I did…

This is the third of three stories.

The thirst one was 'The Feminizing Step-Mother!

The second one was 'My Sep-Mommy Feminized Me!

And now we have this one.

Zowie!

Shiela has opened a dungeon in suburbia, and, man, the clients are flocking.

But also flocking are the police. Durn police. All they do is go around looking for trouble!

Well, they'll find it if they mess with our favorite dominatrix, or her sidekick, who is the world's first and only 'Transinatrix.'

Hey! I made that word up! Pretty clever, eh?

STAY HORNY!

Gracie

Part One

"How are we going to do this?" asked Lucas.

Lucas was wearing his favorite, red dress. It didn't quite fit his big bosom, but that's the way he liked it. He wanted his breasts to flow over the low hem. He wanted his boobs to look like the Grand Canyon. He wanted his hard nipples to push at the material, to create little bumps, little shadows that drew the attention of lookie loos.

"Come in here and I'll show you," said Shiela. She was wearing a peignoir, pale, see through, and held out like a tent by her mammoth mammaries.

Lucas walked into the living room. He glanced at himself in the big mirror in the foyer and smiled. He was getting good at shadowing his eyes, and his lips had responded wonderfully to botox treatments. Add to that the fact that the hormones were really kicking in, and his body was scrump diddly umptious. A round ass, a tight waist, and his face had been feminized.

"Come on, you narcissistic pig," laughed Shiela.

She sat down at the table and powered up the computer.

The living room had been set up for a meet and greet and take the customer's money.

People would enter through the front door and be greeted by Shiela or Lucas. Unable to take their eyes off their hostesses bodies and boobs and butts and immaculately made up faces, they would be guided into the living room.

How are you, how did you hear of us, you can pay cash at the table with the computer on it.

Then, when enough people were sitting in the living room and chatted up, the front door would be closed, the security precautions would kick in, and business would start.

Lucas knew all this. He was just curious about the book keeping. If he was going to be taking money he wanted to know how to handle it, what records to make, and so on.

He sat down next to Shiela and Shiela opened up the computer file used for book keeping.

She explained how to make an entry, how the book keeper program would make a copy and send it to a server off site.

"Why off site?" he asked.

Shiela sat back and pursed her lips. "Well, we know the police will eventually pay attention to us."

"But I thought we were off grid, so to speak, in an unincorporated part of the county?"

She looked at him wryly. "Do you seriously think that a little thing like breaking the law will stop the police?"

"Oh."

Shiela continued. "And behind the police are the politicians, and we have to have all sorts of safeguards in place."

"Okay."

She finished explaining the book keeping, then they went through the kitchen and into the garage.

The door to the basement was in the corner of the garage, and they had set up several security features.

First, there was a little maze of doors leading to the door to the basement.

Second, the door to the basement was now looking like a wall, made of brick, and it was kept in place at all times…until they needed to access the basement.

Third, they had managed to get a clerk in the hall of records to replace the original blueprints for the house with their own 'doctored' blueprints.

Between these things, and a lot of other little things, they were pretty secure in their business.

They walked down into the basement and inspected the furniture.

Chains on the walls. Chastity tubes. St Andrew's Crosses, a rack, and all manner of other little 'toys.'

"Okay," said Lucas. "I guess we're ready for business."

Shiela stood next to him, her hand cupping and rubbing his butt cheek. "Are you going to the doctor tomorrow?"

He nodded.

"Okay. That's the last thing. I'll start putting out advertisements. We should have our first customers tomorrow evening."

"So soon?"

"Absolutely. Don't underestimate John Q. Public's need for sexual discipline."

She chuckled, kissed him soundly, which excited his libido, but didn't make his cock stand up.

Lucas's stand up days were over. He was on testosterone blockers, and his cock had shrunken to a mere couple of inches. Add to that that he was on Depo Provera, a birth control medicine that took the lead out of the pencil, and he was not only small but limp.

But, oh, so horny!

They left the dungeon and set the security features in motion.

Walls in the garage shifted. The brick wall slid down over the door to the basement. The computer sent its final message of the day to the remote server, and they walked up stairs arms around each others waists.

They entered the bedroom and Lucas got undressed. Shiela just stripped her peignoir off and, balled it up, and tossed it onto a chair.

Lucas took off his dress and his bra. His breasts were truly enormous, and Shiela was almost jealous looking at him. He had grown so much in the last few weeks.

He smiled at her and lowered his sissy panties.

Sissy panties had a little stretchy pouch in the front for sissies to place their little packages. The pouch kept them nice and tight and restrained.

Of course come the the morrow Lucas wasn't going to need the sissy panties.

But now, taking the panties down his legs, his little penis flopped out.

"Come here, honey," cooed Shiela.

He walked to her, strutting proudly, but the pride was for his chest, not his groin.

He crawled up and straddled Shiela, his little penis hanging almost between her breasts.

She took it on hand, and his little marbles in the other. She leaned forward and took his peeny in her mouth. It was an automatic deep throat now.

She gobbled him, watched his eyes as he enjoyed the pleasure, then she spat him out and laughed. "You don't even miss your big honker, do you?"

"Not even," he agreed, moving over and to the side of her.

They kissed then. Softly, gently, nibbling away at each others mouths as they fondled each others breasts.

Shiela was wet. Having him so petite and cute down there made her about as horny as a body could get. She was so wet that she sometimes wore a panty liner to absorb her juices.

Lucas, in spite of the fact that he couldn't get hard, and that he was so small, was also super horny. He could only cum when she drained him, and she was sparse with that favor.

She pushed him back and took in air. "Wow." Then, "Are you ready?"

"Are you going to drain me?"

"Oh, don't ask. Not only do I not know, I don't care."

He felt a thrill as she spoke so inconsequentially of his sexual pleasure.

"Just get a couple of strap ons out and let's see.

Two strap ons. She would screw him, but she was in the mood to be screwed herself.

He grinned. He had no desire to screw her, but he absolutely loved it when he brought her to an orgasm.

He jumped off the bed and opened the lower drawer on her side table. He dug around through all the toys and brought out two harnesses.

He slipped one on and fastened it, and Shiela slid off the bed and put one on.

"Which dildos?" she asked slyly.

This was almost a test. She wanted to see what size and length, what shape and texture, he wanted.

Sometimes she would give him what he wanted, but sometimes she would do the opposite.

He chose a big black one with a rubbery texture. It would need lots of lube, but the bulbous shape on the end would tickle his prostate and release his semen. He handed it to her and she merely raised eyebrows lasciviously and snapped it onto the harness.

He took out a big, stiff, glass one for him to use on her.

He knew she loved the way glass felt inside her pussy. He would only put a little lube on it, and it would pull almost painfully on her inner walls, then her own juices would flow, if they weren't already, and it was slip and slide time.

"I think I need to get a bigger one for you," she said as he hopped up on the bed.

"Promises, promises," he chided, and he went onto all fours and awaited her pleasure.

She wasn't about to give him pleasure, at least not so easily.

"Haven't you ever heard of foreplay?" She slapped his ass hard and made him turn around and face her.

She fucked his mouth then, sliding the big dildo in and out. She was teaching him how to deep throat, and he took almost half of the giant intruder into his mouth.

"Good," she said, and she turned him onto his back.

He looked up at her, upside down, and she began to crawl over him.

The glass dildo dragged through his hair, then he was looking up at her piercings.

She had four big, thick rings on each labium, and he pulled her labs apart and began exercising his tongue.

She moaned and went down on his black, misshapen dong.

They couldn't feel their cocks, but it was the idea that excited them. These things strapped around their waists were about to be plummeted home.

While they munched on each other Shiela began playing with his little balls. These were going to be gone, too, on the morrow, and she wanted to enjoy them one last time.

She took them in her mouth and rolled them around. Then she had everything in her mouth, and she could hardly move for the way he was pulling her pussy apart and sliding his tongue around.

"Fuck me," she growled, having had enough.

He wasn't strong anymore. His male muscles were a poor memory, and he hadn't had much muscle to begin with. So she moved with him, helped him manipulate her, and that gave her a thrill.

She liked being stronger than a man.

She turned him around then buried her shaft in him. They were face to face, her holding his legs up in a V, and she watched his face twist with sex happiness.

She lowered her head, pushed his legs back and allowed herself more entry, then she began licking his large, plump lips.

Bent over, he was having trouble breathing. But, actually, she was taking his breath away.

For long minutes and she watched his face grit and grimace and grin. Then she suddenly pulled out, slapped his legs down, and jumped upwards on his body. She settled down on the glass pecker and felt the glass tug at her soft tissues. In a way, it was like her pink insides were bing pulled, ripped, but that was an illusion. They were just clinging, too unfamiliar surfaces, until her pussy generated enough juice to make everything slippery.

Now slippery, she began to shimmy on the tool, gasping, and rocking back and forth.

Lucas reached up and twisted her nipples to the edge of pain, and when she snarled at him he gave an extra twist.

She slapped him, and for an instant he thought he was going to cum.

But, no. That wasn't enough. So he did it again, and again, until Shiela was happy and sexed up and irritated and going out of her mind.

That was when the sex started to get out of control…in the best possible way.

The next morning Lucas awoke early. He put on a teddy and headed for the kitchen. He liked to fix Shiela breakfast.

She didn't demand it, she just hinted, and Lucas, being a true sub, was happy to oblige.

It gave him great purpose to serve her.

He fixed Eggs Benedict, a favorite of Shiela's, and French toast. Adding a glass of apple juice, he trotted up the steps in his high heels and pranced down the hall.

He was becoming quite accomplished in walking in heels. He had sure had a rough time of it at first, but now walking was easy peasy.

"Oh, honey, thank you," Shiela murmured, sitting up so he could place the tray over her thighs.

She ate and he watched her. He loved to watch her. He loved to watch her so much that she had had to tell him to cool it.

After all, in the bathroom?

"Are you getting ready for the doctor?"

"I am."

"Excellent. Tell her you decided to take the testosterone blockers and the depo provera."

"I will."

After washing the dishes, while Shiela was working on the computer on an ad campaign for their new business, Lucas went upstairs and got dressed.

He slipped into a bra, knew he was going to have to go up a cup size, and panties. He wore a simple summer dress. A print pattern with birds on blue, and made his face up.

Shiela had asked him if he wanted permanent make up, but he didn't think so.

Women get permanent make up so they won't have to put it on every day. But he liked putting it on!

He loved to powder his face, to brush his eyelids, and especially to paint his lips.

This day, however, he went light on the make up, then took his time and brushed his hair.

He had had his nails done just a couple of days before, so he was good to go.

He kissed Shiela on the way out and headed for the medical clinic.

Shiela was totally focused on her advertising campaign. The main thing was going to be a series of advertisements, not couched as advertisements, on Facebutt.

She didn't want to take out advertisements because a) they would cost, and b) Facebutt would then have control over them. The trick was to make an ad that didn't look like an ad, get people to visit a website, and avoid all entanglements with tech companies and all their rules and regulations.

She had had the website in place for a few weeks, and it was strictly dark web kind of stuff. It was hard to trace, and she had several safeguards in place. If anybody tried to hack it would reset and ban the hacker.

And she had multiple other gimmicks in place to protect not just the website, but hers and Lucas's identities.

Heck, they weren't doing anything illegal, they were just looking for consenting adults.

But she knew that once they started making money the police would come calling. And behind the police were the crooked politicians.

So she buried herself in algorithms and safety precautions and the morning slowly passed.

Lucas was shown to the exam room by a nurse. She was pretty, but not nearly as pretty as him, and he could detect her jealousy.

He sat down and waited, and the doctor shortly appeared.

The Doc was a good looking woman, slightly thick, but a really nice face and a large set of fun pillows.

"How are you?" the Doc shook hands.

Lucas chatted with her, gave her Shiela's messages, and then they got down to business.

"Disrobe and hop up on the table," said the Doc.

Lucas pulled his panties off and sat on the table.

"Lie back."

Lucas did, and the doctor's narrow fingers gently handled his manhood.

"Wonderful," the doctor commented at one point. She pulled his penis out to three inches, rolled his little testicles, and nodded happily.

"Better living through chemistry, eh?"

Lucas agreed, and the doctor wheeled a tray to the table. She coated his package with disinfectant and rubbed it in thoroughly.

"I'm so glad you decided on this," said the doctor. "Penises can be fun, but in the hands of the wrong man," she suppressed a shiver.

There were small straps on the side of the table and the doctor wrapped them around Lucas's ankles to keep his legs apart.

She made a small incision on his perineum, that spot between the balls and the asshole. She made a small incision on his penis right below the head, then placed the two incisions against each other and began stitching them together.

"I did this for a well endowed man once, and his penis was so long it stuck out behind him. He got very excited just by the act of sitting down."

"What happened to him?"

He did't wipe properly, got material all over his glans. His penis got infected and we eventually had to cut it off."

"You castrated him?"

The doctor didn't even look up. "That's the word for it."

Then, halfway done, the doctor pushed Lucas's balls up into his pubic area, straight up into the little pocket from whence they had originally dropped. Then she pulled his penis tight and completed the stitching.

She had worked fast and efficient, and there was no blood.

"There we go," the doctor smiled and looked up. "Make sure you tell your family and friends if they need anything like this."

Lucas grinned and said he would, then he got dressed and left.

Lucas arrived home just as Shiela finished her first batch of advertising.

"Look at this!" Shiela called to him.

Lucas stepped out of the foyer, faced her and lifted his dress, and called back, "Look at this!"

Shiela stared, and a slow grin spread across her face. "Oh, My, God!"

Shiela came around the table and reached down for Lucas's dick. Except he didn't have a dick anymore. His front was flat, the balls up and the penis stretched back to keep them up and in place.

"God, it's like a pussy with out the slit!"

"And it feels good!" blurted Lucas, taking Shiela's hand and pressing it against his new mons.

"It feels like a pussy, just, you know…no slit."

"We could paint one on?"

"Now there's an idea. Now, I hate to stop admiring you, but come see the advertisement."

Lucas followed her around the table and sat down in front of the computer.

Come tour my dungeon!

Pictures of them, their faces blotted out.

DungeonsRus(dot)com

That was the first ad. There were others. Ads with whips and chains, beautiful women, hints and teasing language.

"These will go out on Facebutt in random order, utilizing different accounts."

"Then they go to the website."

"That's our first layer of security. We get a bit information, we check to see if they are real people, or the police or whoever. They, in turn, get the sales spiel. They learn what we do, what our prices are, and they learn that to get in on the game they are going to have to pass our inspection."

"Won't we lose people?"

"Sure, but there are always more people. Sex never gets old."

Lucas perused the website. He saw pictures of the dungeon. He saw descriptions of the furniture and how they worked. They had price lists by the hour and by the toy.

There were some very intricate descriptions of what was going to be done and how much it would cost.

"Wow. We're expensive!"

"And we're worth it."

"You don't think the prices will drive people away?"

"Nah. Rich people don't mind paying for what they want."

Lucas took a page out of Shiela's book. "And sex is what they want."

"Absolutely."

"And what do we do when they ask to come see our dungeon?"

"We check them out. We use those People Finder websites and see if they are who they really say they are."

"Then what?"

"Then we arrange a time, gather everybody together and bring them here, and...part-ay!"

"Isn't that going to be a lot of work?"

"Nah. The computer checks them out. We'll eventually hire somebody to drive a van. We'll put electronic counter surveillance measures on the van...it's going to be as smooth as silk."

"You've convinced me. So ads are out now?"

"Yep. Just before you came home. As soon as I get some responses I'll check them out. I hope that by tonight we'll have our first customers."

By that time it was time for lunch, and the two girls walked into the kitchen. They chatted about prices and ways to insure customers were real and not cops.

And they talked about Lucas's new 'pussy.'

"I swear. That is exactly like a mons. It is perfect!"

"I love the way it feels. I feel more confidence just walking."

"What's it like walking?"

"Oh, Lord, that's the interesting part. I didn't expect this when I researched it, but the head of my peeny is between my thighs, and when I walk my thighs brush against my head. Just walking makes me hornier and hornier. It feels like I could just walk for a while and cum."

They were eating tuna sandwiches and drinking Negronis. Negronis weren't tasty, but they were simple, and they were unique. The recipe was:

1 oz gin

1 oz Campari

1 oz sweet vermouth

Orange peel garnish

Neither girl was a fan of gin, a working mans drink from England's industrial revolution which tasted like motor oil and flat soda water.

But by experimenting with the ingredients and portions one could come up with a variety of different but very potent drinks.

For an hour after eating the tuna fish they played with different drinks, and in the end they agreed they still didn't like gin, but they liked the drink. Weird.

Then the computer chimed.

DING!

The girls looked at each other, then jumped up and ran into the living room.

Hi, My name is Tim. My wife (Marsha) and I are intrigued by your dungeon and would consider a tour. What do we have to do to make this work?

Shiela sat down and typed:

Hi, Tim. It is wonderful to meet you. My name is Shiela, and I will be your contact. We need to know your place of business. With that information we will do a very discreet background check. Be assured, nobody will even know we are looking at you.

After we have your place of business give us a half hour and we will let you know the next step in this procedure. In the meantime, do you have any experience with dungeons? Dominatrices, or such things?

Shiela sent the message. Then went into the kitchen to make another drink. Before she was back Tim had responded with his full name and place of business.

Shiela, Tim here, and I appreciate your discretion. Our full names are Timothy and Marsha Van Deering. I am co-owner of Latex Products Inc.

He had included a telephone number and the address of himself and his company. He had also included a list of a half a dozen experiences, which experiences were with high class and even notorious BDSM concerns.

He had listed a couple of ranches, a couple of dominatrices, and OWK.

"Holy zowbadeechy!" exclaimed Shiela.

"What's a zowbadeechy?"

Shiela didn't bother explaining, probably couldn't, but said, "OWK, Other World Kingdom. That's overseas and big. It's a whole country of BDSM."

"A whole country?"

"It's not big, but it has its own currency, flag, laws, everything. This guy has been places and seen things. We'd better be real professional with him."

With that Shiela acknowledged Tim, then fed his name, and Marsha's name, into a People Finder. Within minutes the computer had given them everything they needed, including criminal records, photos, and past addresses, phone numbers…everything.

The girls high fived, then Shiela set about making inquiries.

She called the company Tim worked for and found out he had started the company seven years earlier and was the co-president.

She checked with his high school, then his college.

From there she got other hints, and within 15 minutes she had a complete dossier on Tim and Marsha.

Satisfied that he was legit, she sent him a message.

Tim! We have very carefully checked to make sure you are who you say you are, and that you are not connected with the police or any other party pooper agency. This is for our common protection. Nobody likes a party pooper.

We would like to invite you to experience our dungeon.

We will send a limousine to pick you and your wife up at seven o'clock tonight. We will return you home at approximately twelve. Please don't eat a heavy meal before you come, and we will have liquid refreshments for you when you arrive. Wear clothes that you don't mind losing.

Looking forward to meeting you in the flesh. ;o)

Shiela.

At seven o'clock Lucas drove the rented limousine to the home address of Tim and Marsha Watson.

Their home was in the hills, at the top of a long, circular drive that had a steep drop off on one side, and a beautifully overgrown woods on the other side.

The house came into view. It was modern, but done in the old Hollywood style, Mediterranean, with lots of bushes in the front. He could see part of a large swimming pool and a raised garden in the back.

He drove to the front of the house and Tim and Marsha popped out the front door and descended a series of shallow steps.

Lucas stepped out of the limo and greeted them and held the door open for them. He was wearing a skin tight, black, latex dress. It was so tight his nipples could be seen through the material, and the Watson inspected his form happily.

"Very nice," said Tim. "Are you Shiela.

Lucas, nervous as hell, kept himself under control. "I'm Lucas."

Marsha glanced at her husband and they exchanged a look. It wasn't good or bad, just significant.

The Watsons were beautiful people. They were in Cross Fit condition and in their late forties. Tim's hair was prematurely grey, but arranged in a stylish fifty's manner. Marsha's hair was in the French fashion, piled and golden and very sexy.

Lucas couldn't wait to see what she would look like when that hair came down.

Lucas started the trip down the drive and Tim asked, "Your name. Are you trans? Or…?"

"Trans," replied Lucas. "Freshly made." He wanted to ask if that was a problem, but Shiela had said to keep his mouth shut and let people develop their own thoughts and attitudes.

"Wonderful," murmured Marsha with a wide smile.

"How interesting. We've been to a few soirees, but I don't believe we've ever, uh, had doings with a trans person. Are you involved or just driving?"

"Oh, I'm involved." He smiled into the rear view mirror.

"And may we be inquisitive as to your, uh…trans-ity?"

"Of course," Lucas was almost shaking, He was actually scared. He had never thought he would react that way, but…there it was.

Still, the Watsons were very pleasant and personable.

"Normally we wouldn't be so nosy, but your condition, and our inexperience, inspires our curiosity.

Inexperience, hunh! This couple obviously had tons of experience. They were just nice people about it all.

"So do you still have your original equipment?"

"I do, but it's not obvious."

"How so?"

Lucas explained how his penis was shrunken and limp and tucked back between his legs by surgery.

"Oh, Lord," whispered Marsha. She made a squirming motion and Lucas realized that she had lifted her dress and started playing with herself.

Tim chuckled. "You have properly excited my wife. She often prefers women, and to have a man that is a women, if you will forgive my clumsy labeling, it is quite stimulating to her. Correct, my dear."

"Absolutely."

Marsha was staring at the back of Lucas's head.

"And, if I may ask, tell me to to shut up if I cross any boundaries, how do you pee?"

"Sitting down."

"And did you ever wear a chastity tube prior to your current situation?"

"I did, but I much prefer the current arrangement. It provides sexual stimulation without the uncomfortableness."

"And how do you like sex?" blurted Marsha.

"Quite well," quipped Lucas, and they all laughed. Then Lucas said, "I prefer anal. I much prefer it."

"And would you be averse to my pleasuring you?"

Shiela had told Lucas this would happen. And it would happen soon.

"In all honesty?" Lucas raised his eyes to Tim in the mirror.

"Of course."

"I am a virgin in that respect."

Tim caught his breath.

"My partner, Shiela, has made it clear to me that that is not going to be an option. But, I have to tell you, she is planning a lottery, a very expensive lottery, as to who shall deflower me."

"Oh, Lord," and Tim sat back. It was obvious he had a hand in his crotch.

"And, please…don't cum. Either of you. We have a full night of fun and games and would prefer that you are at a peak."

"Of course not!" Marsha almost sounded offended.

They drove through town, it was an hour long trip, and they chatted happily. By the time Lucas arrived at his house they were as old friends, and Lucas had learned a lot.

Tim's company was quite prosperous, and he and Marsha were quite adventurous. They were also a bit disappointed in their experiences.

"Do you remember that bald transvestite?" commented Marsha cheerfully, but displaying a sort of disparagement.

"The one who thought being bald would turn you on? Oh, that was funny." Tim spoke to Lucas. "I wouldn't even call him a transvestite, he was a wanna be drag queen, quite ludicrous, and he actually started shaving his hair off while we…"

They were all laughing as Lucas pulled up to the house.

Lucas opened the back door and the Watsons stepped out and looked around.

"Nice," murmured Tim.

"Sedate," breathed Marsha, glancing at the sparsity of houses, the good landscaping of the neighborhood.

Then they walked up the walk, climbed a few steps, crossed the porch, and entered the house.

Part Two

Shiela greeted the effusively, but with professional restraint. She showed them into the living room, took their outer apparel and seated them.

"Just a few minutes of paperwork and we'll be ready to start."

Payment was taken care of expeditiously and Lucas served them their drinks of choice. Aunt Roberta.

Lucas had been learning about the more exotic drinks, and he had looked up the Aunt Roberta, as it was supposed to be the strongest drink in the world.

It had supposedly been invented by the daughter of a slaveowner 150 years before. Roberta apparently ran away from her abusive parents, turned to prostitution, then making moonshine.

The drink consisted of gin, vodka, brandy, blackberry liqueur and absinthe.

Lucas made the drinks quickly and professionally and Tim watched carefully. He was satisfied with Lucas's work as a bartender for he smiled and lifted the glass to him when he was served.

Then, it was time to work.

Shiela clicked the buttons on the keyboard which changed the house from a house into a place of play.

Bolts shot in the doors so no one could get in. The windows were already bolted.

The brick wall in the garage rose up to reveal a solid metal door with imposing rivets on it.

The lights dimmed and Shiela led Tim by the hand through the kitchen into the garage. Marsha followed, her arm around Lucas's waist.

Lucas could tell that the older woman really wanted him.

They entered the garage and turned to the right. They went through a regular door and stepped into a small six by six room, and the floor started rotating. It move slowly, there was light music, a bit of Pink Floyd, then the door stopped.

Tim and Marsha had no idea in which direction they were facing now.

Shiela pressed a remote and one wall slid upwards to reveal the iron dungeon door.

Tim was impressed by the security features. "Wonderful," he stated under his breath.

They all walked down the steps into the dungeon.

Lucas had been working on the ambience. The walls looked aged, the ceiling fixtures hung by a single line and the glow of the bulbs was properly spooky.

It was simple stuff, but it didn't look cheesy, instead gave a real feel of menace.

One expected Torquemada to jump out and say 'boo!'

Shiela suddenly turned to Tim and pressed her body up against his. She was in black leather, mesh stockings, and her boobs looked positively enormous.

Tim kissed back, and grunted when she grabbed his jewels.

"So you like it rough, eh?" She lifted and a crazed look came into Tim's eyes. Then she began to undress him. She ripped buttons, pinched his nipples, and kept laughing and kissing and laughing and…Tim had an unusually large member, and it filled her hand nicely.

Meanwhile, Lucas let Marsha watch the activities for a moment, felt her getting hot as her husband was manhandled and sexed up. Then he gently touched her hand, moved it to his breast.

Marsha's eyes glinted, she turned to him, pulled his breast out of the dress and began to suck it.

Then she kissed Lucas, and it was obvious that she was very hungry. Lucas was a man, who was a girl, and she liked girls, and…

"That's enough," whispered Shiela, pushing Tim away. "Come with me."

Mid kiss, their faces twisted, keeping their lips locked, Lucas and Marsha watched as Shiela led Tim to the rack.

Marsha broke the kiss, turned and watched, and Lucas moved behind her, held her, massaged her breasts, and they watched.

For Lucas the spanking and the hot paste was old stuff, though still exciting.

For Marsha, it was something more. Her breath caught, and Lucas just knew she was thinking about doing some of this at home. He whispered the recipe of the paste to her, and told her she had to make his spanking peak, then it would be most effective.

Watching her husband cry out, writhe in sexual pain, and lurch about was downright therapeutic for Marsha.

Lucas asked, "Is he always on top?"

She nodded.

"But you'd like to try it."

She nodded again. She was licking her lips and her hand went down to her groin and started rubbing.

"Come on, let's put you on a machine."

But it wasn't a machine so much as a fuck pole. Lucas moved a plate with a pole standing up on it. On top of the pole was a nice sized dildo.

Lucas helped Marsha out of her clothes, then placed her on the plate and moved the dildo up into her, then locked it in place.

Marsha's eyes went wide. This wasn't a serious toy, but it was serious enough for her. She couldn't take a step in any direction. She was dick locked.

But Lucas wasn't done.

He put clothes pins on her nipples, then stood beside her and massaged her anus with his fingers. All the time he nibbled on her ears, kissed her neck, whispered dirty things to her.

She loved it. She was forced to watch her husband cry out as the heat built on his ass, her pussy was stretched and her asshole stimulated, and then there was the loving touches of Lucas.

Shiela had taken Tim about as far as he could go. He was sobbing, and she unbuckled him and moved him to a bench.

Lucas had been on this bench a few times, and he knew what Tim was going through.

Tim's forearms and lower legs were restrained, his face was on a little platform so he could only look forward. Shiela moved a machine behind him and centered it on his ass. She turned the machine on and a big dildo plunged in and out, in and out.

Now all of this was good, but normally it wouldn't have been enough. The burning ass, the heinie fucker, the way Tim was imprisoned, it could be handled by a man with will and discipline, and Tim had that will and discipline.

But what Tim couldn't handle was the fact that Shiela cared.

He wasn't left to ponder, he wasn't distracted by whips. He was kissed.

Shiela simply sat in front of him and kissed him, and spoke to him in a sweet, loving tone. She talked about men and their needs, and how selfish they could be. She talked about how he had misjudged and mistreated his wife.

Tim began to sob. This wasn't just rock 'em sock 'em BDSM, it was up close and personal, down into the home of the soul.

Standing with her pussy trapped by a penis, Marsha could hear every word spoken. She listened as Shiela excoriated him with kisses, reached into his very soul and twisted the truth into him like a knife.

And she began to cry.

It was true.

Shiela had analyzed this couple perfectly.

Then Shiela turned to Lucas. "Put a dildo on her."

Tim looked around wildly, his face trying to get free of the little platform it was on. He suddenly knew what was about to happen.

Yet Shiela turned back to him, whispered, kissed, and slowly convinced him that this was right, that he had to do this, that he owed it to Marsha.

Lucas lowered the penis pole and helped Marsha walk over to a cabinet. He took out a strap on and buckled it on her waist, then he asked, "Pick a dildo. Pick out one you think he'll like.

Marsha didn't have to ask who 'he' was. She picked out a rather large one with a string of bulbs up the shaft.

Lucas snapped the dildo into the harness, then led Marsha to a spot behind Tim and waited.

Shiela nodded, and Lucas greased the dildo, then he had Marsha grease Tim.

"Lots of lube," he murmured softly. "You don't want him to feel the pain, you want him to feel the love. You want him to beg for this later on. Got it?"

Marsha did. A firm light in her eyes, she gently reamed Tim out.

Tim knew what was going to happen. He had been screwed in the butt before, but not by his wife.

If his wife screwed him he knew he would lose a certain amount of stature in her eyes. He would lose a bit of the power he held over her.

It scared him.

But Shiela had prepared him well.

Shiela looked over Tim to Lucas and gave a nod.

Lucas moved Marsha forward. He placed the tip of her penis in the right place, then he placed a hand on her buns and pushed.

Tim arched, and cried out, and knew that his life would never be the same.

But within a few moments he realized that that was all right. He was married, and Marsha did have certain rights, after all.

Lucas gave the Watsons a ride home. They sat quietly in the back seat, arms around each other, and pondered what had happened.

He was experienced, and now so was she.

He was broken in, and she had ridden her first rodeo, and she liked it.

Lucas pulled up in front of their house and opened the door for them.

They were weak. They had gone places they didn't expect, and they were never going to be the same.

Lucas helped them as they mounted the steps and entered the house.

They didn't say anything as he helped them up the stairs to their bedroom.

They were mute, but grateful—Lucas could tell that from the gratitude shining from their eyes—when he helped them get undressed and into bed.

Then Lucas turned off the lights and showed himself out.

He was nervous, but not for the same reasons he had been nervous earlier.

Shiela had taken the couple further than Lucas had thought possible, and he had learned a lot of things, but he was asking himself the question: how far is too far?

He felt they had gone far beyond too far, yet…he thought everything was okay.

The next day Shiela and Lucas slept in, and when they came downstairs they found several messages waiting for them.

Two were from the website, newbies.

One was from Tim.

Two others were from people they had never heard of, but not through the website.

Shiela opened Tim's first.

Dearest Shiela and lovely Lucas. I…we…have never had such an in depth experience in our lives. You have truly changed our lives.

I have advised two of our friends of your amazing services, and they should be contacting you shortly. I vouch for them personally, they have been friends for years, and they share common interests with myself and my wife.

I will leave a commendation on your website, and please contact me if there is anything I can do for you.

Again, thank you.

Tim Watson

Two names were appended.

Shiela and Lucas turned to each other with big grins. They high fived, then Shiela turned back to the messages.

She opened two messages from the people who Tim had recommended. They asked for a tour and gave their names, addresses, and even a list of some of the dominatrixes and BDSM ranches they had been to.

Shiela started the People Finder process, then opened the other two messages.

One was a serious inquiry, and she answered and gave the conditions necessary.

The other message simply said, *You will burn in hell!*

Lucas stared, and was bothered.

Shiela just grunted and quipped, "I hope old scratch has some good ass paste."

Then Lucas snickered. He knew that Shiela was right, and she had warned him such things would happen.

Some people don't like sex. Some people don't like other people to have sex. Some people would have to be ignored.

They put that email address on the blocked list. He wouldn't even be able to access their website. Assuming it was a he. It might be a she.

When the procedures had started, Shiela sat back and clasped her hands behind her head. "Well, it looks like we have a business."

Lucas nodded, then asked, "Does doing this…did that scene last night…"

"Yes?"

"Did it turn you on?"

For answer Shiela grabbed Lucas's hand and dragged him upstairs.

The business was started, and when the people who Tim had recommended came for their tour Shiela and Lucas found out something very interesting.

Tim's company, LTI, or Latex Products Incorporated, specialized in sex toys!

That's right! Tim made dildos and vibrators and portable pussies for men and sex dolls and whips and…and everything. He had even started looking into making furniture.

After the two friends he had recommended to Shiela and Lucas reported back with glowing reviews he emailed Shiela.

Dear Shiela, my ass still glows with love for you.

My friends were most enthusiastic over your services. I sent them to you to be sure, even though I was sure, if that makes sense.

I would like to put a link to your website on my website.

Also, as we develop latex products, I would like to enlist you as a product tester and reviewer.

Again, thank you, and Marsha sends her love to dear Lucas.

BTW, when is the lottery going to take place?

Yours forever

Tim

Shiela was excited by the proposed possibilities here. By being on the Latex Products website they wouldn't have to advertise much, if at all, and they would still have a steady source of customers. And the idea of being a product tester for the latest cutting edge sex toys, now that was a dream job come true.

She was confused, however, by the reference to a 'lottery.'

"Lucas? Do you know anything about a lottery?"

Lucas's face turned a little red. "Well, I made it up. I admitted to them, on the drive over here, that I was a virgin. Tim showed interest and I was a little scared, so I made up something about a lottery for my virginity to distract him."

"Heck, that didn't distract him, it focused him. You realize you're going to have to put out now, don't you?"

"You mean do it with a man?"

Shiela lifted an eyebrow.

"But I don't like men! I don't even want to kiss them!"

"We can get around the kissing. We can put you on a bench with a ball gag, or better, a penis gag. But you'll have to take a real penis."

Lucas looked very worried now.

"Hey, it's not much different than a plastic pecker. Just softer and warmer, and it spits."

"But…a man?"

"Hey, you're the one who thought this lottery thing up. Besides, it's a great marketing device! What man wouldn't want to deflower a virgin?"

"But I'm a guy…I mean, underneath it all!"

"That's even better, to deflower a trans, that's every man's real dream."

"I thought men wanted to deflower female type virgins!"

"They only think they do. Let me tell you a nasty, little secret."

"What?"

"Women like women, and men like men. Underneath it all."

"But—"

Shiela held up a hand to forestall complaint. "I know, and man on woman will never die. It is crucial to replenishing the human race. But we've reached a point where the man/woman dynamic isn't so important. Now it's okay to let your true feelings, your real desires, to flourish. Do you know how many men are turning homo? How many women are lesbian? Heck, you're living proof of the sexual truth and times we are traveling through."

Lucas was silent after that. It was a lot to think about.

And he had to think about his ass, too. He loved it when Shiela had deflowered him with her fake penis, and he lived to be drained by her. But to be turned out, to be made available to men. Even without the kissing stuff…ech!

A week passed. There were only a couple of weeks until Grant, Lucas's father, was due home.

But business was booming.

"What are we going to do when my father comes home?" Lucas asked at one point.

"I don't know. You know, at first I just wanted to strike out, to abuse him, but now I'm making money, my own money, and I have different feelings.

"I'm no longer pissed off at him, or men in general. Heck, I'm doing what they wanted to do to me, and have done to me, for my whole life.

"So, I don't know. Maybe we'll move. Pick up our torture toys and start a ranch out in the country or something. Or maybe an accommodation can be worked out. He is a lawyer, after all, and he didn't get rich by being unworkable."

Lucas grunted. "He once told me that the only difference between a lawyer and a crook is one of perspective."

"Well, he's certainly not dumb, is he."

So a week had passed, and they were working hard, when the doorbell rang.

DING DONG!

Shiela pulled up the security cam and saw two cops standing on the front porch.

Shiela didn't hesitate. She pressed a key on the computer and bolts shot in doors, the brick wall came down in the garage, and all information was sent to a remote server.

On the porch the cops heard the sound of the bolts snicking and they looked at each other. Then one pounded on the door.

Shiela, fortunately was dressed, as was Lucas. They walked to the front door, drew the bolts, and opened it a crack. "Yes?"

"Police, ma'am. May we come in?"

Shiela pondered briefly. Technically, she was supposed to demand a warrant. But to make a demand was to invite suspicion. Besides, she knew everything was locked down, and all the police would find would be her drawer of toys next to the bed.

"Just a moment." She closed the door and fiddled with the chain. As she made the rattling noise she said to Lucas. "Act stupid. Don't worry."

She undid the chain and opened the door and stood back.

It was male cop and female cop. The male cop was tall and built, the female cop was chunky, but built. They both looked like they worked weights. They were both very spiffy in their cleaned and pressed uniforms.

"What's this all about, officers? Come on in and have a seat."

She led them into the living room and indicated a couch.

The officers sat down, and their eyes were all over the place. Trying to be subtle, but about as subtle as a tank in a rose garden.

"We, uh…had some complaints. Something about noise, and…do you run a business here?"

"Not really. Not unless you count Ebay." Shiela waved at the computer on the dining room table, which was open to Ebay. "I'm trying to figure out how to make money and this computer stuff is really difficult.

It wasn't, but it established Shiela as somewhat of an airhead.

"Would you guys like a drink?" Lucas tried to sound dumb, and he did pretty well. "We have whiskey and vodka and—"

"We're on duty, ma'am," the male officer spoke, but his eyes went up and down and totally scoped out Lucas.

The female officer took over. "That's funny, we had complaints, but…do you mind if I use your bathroom?"

"Of course. Lucy, do you mind pointing Officer," squint at nameplate,

"Roderiguiz to the upstairs?"

Lucas, now Lucy, was puzzled, why not the downstairs bathroom? But he stood up and took Lucy to the stairs and pointed her upward. "End of the corridor turn left through the bedroom. you'll find it there."

"Thank you," the officer said gratefully, and she started climbing the stairs.

Lucy waited a moment, then turned around. The male officer was in the kitchen with Shiela, and it sounded like he was flirting with her.

Weird.

Lucas sat down at the dining room table and wondered why he was supposed to 'point' the officer upstairs? Why not go to the downstairs? What was going on in Shiela's devious mind?

Then Shiela and the officer came back, and Shiela was walking closely to him, brushing his thigh with hers, and he was red-faced, but smiling.

Flirting, indeed. Who was flirting who?"

A few minutes later Officer Roderiguez descended the stairs, and a few minutes later the two cops were out the front door and walking down the walk towards their cruiser.

Shiela waited a moment, peeked out the front window, and sighed. She plopped down on the couch and stated, "Now we know."

"Now we know what? And why did you let that cop to go upstairs?"

"Well," she suddenly jumped up. "Bourbon and Coke. Let's talk in the other room."

They went into the kitchen and Shiela mixed a couple of plain, old bourbon and Cokes. They settled down at the kitchen table.

"First, did you notice that it took a long time for Officer Roderiguez to shake a bush?"

"I guess it did take her a while."

"She wasn't peeing, she was looking around."

"Then why did you send her up there?"

"Because I wanted her to look around. We've got nothing up there but a drawer of sex toys. Besides, what if she did find something? Anything they found without a search warrant is not admissible. Also, they weren't even in their jurisdiction. If they found anything they would have been in trouble.But they weren't going to find anything."

100

"But why were they here, anyway?"

"Not why, but who? Who sent them in our direction. Was it just a simple look because they saw an ad? Or did one of our customers betray us?"

Lucas was silent at that, and he took a big slug of bourbon.

Cops or not, business was business. For another week Shiela and Lucas picked up people, transported them to the house, took care of paperwork, then went down to the basement.

It was a lot of paperwork and busy work, but it was necessary.

On the good side, their coffers were swelling.

And, Shiela had come up with a lottery for Lucas's butt.

She put out some subtle advertising, and the response was through the roof. Tickets were ten thousand dollars, and people were buying dozens of the tickets in blocks.

Shortly they had over a hundred thousand dollars, and more was coming in.

"Lady," said Shiela, "Your ass is worth real money."

And I use it for shitting," quipped Lucas.

Shiela laughed. "Okay, this Saturday night. Big party. No dungeon, just an upstairs party. We'll have a drawing, and your ass is on the line."

Now Lucas's face looked sober.

Saturday night arrived, along with nearly a hundred people.

Shiela and Lucas knew most of them, and some of the people they didn't know had been invited by friends.

That was okay.

Still, Shiela didn't like not knowing who everybody was.

But, nothing to do about it, they partied. Everybody was in sexy dress, there was lots of fucking in the closets, and even a small orgy in the upstairs bedroom.

Clothes tended to get lost, everybody was drunk, and the drawing was held.

Shiela pulled Lucas to the front of the room and they stood on a couple of chairs. they were both drunk and laughing and Shiela yelled out, "What am I bid for this gorgeous piece of ass?"

People yelled out numbers and ribald comments.

"Never been sullied. A pure vestal virgin if ever there was one!"

Lots of laughter at that, but Lucas was actually feeling a bit embarrassed. But that was okay. It was all for a good cause, his and Shiela's pocket book.

Tim brought over the bowl with the ticket stubs in it. He mixed the stubs up while Shiela blindfolded Lucas.

Lucas placed his hand in the bowl and swirled it around. He selected a stub and lifted it out of the bowl, then handed it to Shiela. The blindfold was taken off and Shiela yelled out, "Johnathon Quisling! Johnny! come up and take your fair maid's hand!"

Johnathon was a big, bulky man with a salesman's grin. He shook a fist in the air and exulted, and Lucas stared up at him and was a little scared.

"Okay. Tomorrow night Johnathon will collect his prize. We will make a recording and it will be on sale on the website. Now, LET'S PARTY!"

And that was the moment the police broke in.

A large crashing sound and the front door flew inward. People screaming as SWAT cops charged in, pushing people, waving their guns, and yelling their cop commands.

"Get down! On the floor!" And so on.

It was a sullen bunch that was sitting on the floor of the living room, the dining room, and even on the steps.

And sullen was going to translate into anger very quickly.

Shiela was identified and pulled to her feet. It was Officer Bascomb and Officer Roderiguez, and now they had a search warrant.

Shiela took the warrant and said, "I don't believe we're in the city limits."

Officer Bascomb didn't care.

"Furthermore, I would like to know what you're looking for?"

"It's on the warrant."

But the warrant was peculiarly vacant on that score.

"You realize that you are violating my civil rights and that I will bring a lawsuit against the department, and against you, Officer Bascomb, and you, Officer Roderiguez, and against the city."

"You can...HEY! Put that cell phone away!"

One of the guests, Johnathon Quisling, was half standing, had his cell phone directed at them.

In his other hand he had his business card.

"Nice try, Officer. This is private property, and we have committed no crime, unless you're really the fun police."

"I said," Bascomb advanced on the Quisling, "Put that..." then he had the business card in front of his eyes.

Johnathon Quisling

Attorney at Law

A sound like 'Urk,' came out of Bascomb's throat. He held the card and he backed up. Quisling was just starting, however.

"I represent these ladies. Let me see that warrant."

Shiela handed him the warrant. She was shocked by everything, holding on, and couldn't believe that she hadn't known Quisling was a lawyer. Of course somebody else had brought him, but, still...

"Officer, this warrant belongs in a shit house. The purpose is vacuous, the items to be searched for are too general, and...who is this Judge Thompkins?"

"Sir, Judge Thompkins is in charge arbitrations in the night court."

"Night court? Arbitrator? He's not even a judge! He's an appointed lawyer for a brief reason. Now collect your soldiers and clear this house. I will be filing injunctions and asking for your arrest for this travesty."

By now the other cops had all stopped their activities. They were shuffling their feet and wondering what to do.

What they did was shuffle on out of there, with Bascomb's tail between his legs.

The cops gone, the party didn't feel like continuing. People slowly gathered their clothes, thanked Shiela and Lucas, and headed out.

Quisling passed his card to Shiela and they stood and chatted for a moment.

"I can't thank you enough. What do I owe you?"

"A good time at your next party."

"Really? I mean, yes, of course, but—"

"Look, I don't mind cops when they stick to their jobs, but you know what all this means, don't you?"

Shiela nodded. "I'm afraid I do."

"Good. So give me a call if you need anything, and you probably will. Tomorrow I'll go raise a ruckus, but I'd prefer to let everything settle down, keep it all for later, if we need it. Okay?"

"Sounds wonderful."

After Johnathon left, and everybody was gone, Lucas asked, "What did he mean, 'do you know what all this means?'"

They sat down and looked at the mess that the party had left. They were sharing a Coke, and Shiela said, "Do you remember that I told you the police would eventually show up?"

"Yes."

"And who's behind the police?"

"I don't know. City Hall? Politicians?"

"Bingo." Shiela pushed a strand of loose hair back over her ear. "Now politicians are notorious cowards. They don't dare do anything because somebody, somewhere, won't like it."

"So what does that mean?"

"What's behind politicians?"

Lucas was blank.

"The people behind the politicians are the ones who own them."

The word sort of squeaked out of Lucas's mouth. "Criminals?"

"I hate to repeat myself, but…Bingo."

Epilogue

The following night Lucas was on the bench. His forearms were in the leather cuffs on front platforms. His ankles were on the back platforms in similar cuffs.

He was naked, but fully make up.

His large breasts hung down and his face was on the front platform, his long hair hanging down the sides of his head.

His buttocks was slightly raised and presented his anus perfectly.

Behind him Shiela was lubing his rectum thoroughly. She spoke to Johnathon, who was lubing up his cock.

"Now, remember, Johnathon. Take your time. If you cum within five minutes we'll let you rest and have another shot. But if you get too rough then everything is off. I don't want you to break Lucas. This is his first time, and…be very, very gentle."

Johnathon nodded. "I will. I'll be so gentle she doesn't even feel me enter her."

Him, her, it was all the same to Lucas. His heart was pounding, he was a couple of drinks to the wind, and his rectum was actually giving little twitches and shivers.

"Okay, are you ready?"

Johnathon nodded.

"Then please step forward and take your prize."

Johnathon held his big, thick cock in one hand and stepped up to Lucas's ass. He touched the tip of his penis to Lucas's brown star, and he began to move forward.
He held his breath, and sunk deeper, and the only sound was Lucas's gentle squeal of delight.

The Step-Mommy and the Lady Boy!
Feminization to BDSM to a final showdown!

Grace Mansfield

A Note from the Author!

Zowie! I love when I finish up a series!

This was great fun, as little Lucas returns home, and his step-mother is ready for him. She trains Lucas, and feminizes him, and transgenders him, then they open a dungeon in the heart of suburbia.

In this, the final story, they expand their house of domination, and run afoul of gangsters, cops, politicians, and just about everything outside of an old ladies' society.

We got everything! BDSM in double the dungeons! Gangsters with big dicks, and a final showdown between everybody that results in... well, in chaos.

Until the final scene when something so unexpected happens both Lucas and Shiela are knocked for a literal loop!

Have fun, and...

STAY HORNY!

Gracie

Part One

"How are you doing?" Shiela came out to the patio carrying two drinks. Simple drinks. Bourbon and Coke with straws.

She was a beautiful woman. Heavy on the breasts, a face that was deceptively innocent, long hair that reflected the sunlight.

Lucas looked up at her and there was a wisdom in his face that had not been there before.

He had been transformed. His penis was shrunken and sewed back between his legs. His balls were up in his groin where they had originally descended from.

He was a woman in every respect but one: he had no pussy.

But that hadn't stopped him from experiencing what a woman experiences. He had been raffled off, awarded to the lottery winner, and experienced his first anal sex with a real, live, warm penis.

It had been interesting, to say the least.

"I'm doing good," he answered.

Shiela handed him his glass and sat on the lounge chair next to him. She watched him, curious as to what was going on in his mind.

He knew she was curious, and he explained, "It was good. A real penis is different, but...I'd prefer dildos and vibrators."

"Why?"

"I don't have any feelings for men. I don't mind them, I don't hate them, I just have preferences."

"Fair enough," Shiela sat back to think about what he had said.

Lucas was thinking about something else though.

Two nights ago when they had raffled Lucas off, and the cops had shown up.

Shown up with a bogus search warrant, out of their jurisdiction, and an attitude.

"What are the police going to do now?"

"I'm not sure," admitted Shiela. She started counting fingers. "Get a real search warrant. Turn it over to another agency, maybe even federal. Ask their bosses what they should do. Cops are just robots. All they do is follow the law, and the law is just a script for controlling people."

They sipped contentedly, worried, but knowing that worry wasn't going to accomplish anything.

"So what do we do?"

"Business as usual. Wait for people to ask for a tour of our dungeon, check them out, invite them over."

Lucas nodded. "It's a shame."

"What's a shame?"

"That the police, and whoever uses them, want to bully us."

"Bullying is just incidental to power, money, the desire to control everything."

"Makes them look pretty small."

"I've never met an honest politician."

Lucas considered her words. "Have you met a lot of politicians?"

"Sure. I had a life before I married your father." She grunted. "He thought he was rescuing me, and I thought so, too. But here I am, doing the same thing, but even more so."

"The same thing? You had a dungeon before?"

"Not so much as a dungeon as whips and things and the desire. This was in Washington, and my clientele were all politicians."

Lucas got up and went in for more drinks. He returned and they sipped, then dipped into the pool, and whiled the morning away. This was an official day off, and they had been working hard. They were ready for a break.

They weren't about to get one, however.

DING DONG!

They looked at each other. They weren't expecting anybody.

They were naked when they went into the house, and dripping wet.

Shiela peeked through the side window.

One man in a suit. Fiftyish. Serious.

Shiela pressed the intercom. "May we help you?"

"Good morning. Am I speaking to Shiela?"

"Who wants to know?"

"My name is Bertrand, and I represent certain political interests."

Shiela glanced at Lucas, who had caught his breath.

"You'll have to give us five minutes, Mr. Bertrand."

"Perfectly fine."

On the porch he turned and leaned against a post. He took out his cell phone and began reading and tapping.

Shiela and Lucas trotted upstairs. They dressed quickly with no attempt at make up or sexy outfits. They had no illusions that Bertrand was there to get his cock sucked.

Seven minutes later Shiela opened the door and Bertrand entered with a smile. "Thanks you."

His voice was deep, his manner pleasant, and he was innocuous. He gave the attitude of an apologetic salesman. He wanted you to like him, and was sorry to intrude on your happiness. Even if it was to bring you more happiness.

"Have a seat, please," Shiela showed him into the front room. "Something to drink?"

"If you have a Coke?"

Lucas headed for the kitchen and Shiela and Bertrand sat opposite each other and smiled.

Lucas returned with three Cokes and they all sat back and sipped.

Shiela started the ball rolling. "And what brings you to us on this fine afternoon?"

"Call me Bert." He settled in, quite professional and self possessed. "It appears that my employers and you got off to a less than desirable start."

"And your employers are?"

"Anonymous. I'm sure you understand."

"As people who wish to remain anonymous ourselves, we do. But that puts us at an impasse. I'm sure you understand."

Bert nodded, then leaped right into it.

"We can't have independent houses. It cuts into our business. We have houses that, even in the short time you've been in business, are suffering financial losses."

"If we have a superior product..." she left the statement open.

"Apparently you do, and we would like to know about that."

"Sorry. Trade secrets."

He smiled for the first time. "Yes." He nodded. "I am prepared to offer substantial sums of money. We wish to buy into your business, buy your expertise, perhaps for you to even to train some of our personnel."

"Since that would be giving away our secret recipes, and since you and I know perfectly well that it would be only a matter of time until your employers would attempt to finagle us out of our business, we will have to decline your offer."

"Well," he placed his Coke on the table. "We'll be in touch." He started to stand up, but Shiela leaned across to him and placed a hand on his knee.

"Are you prepared to entertain a counter offer?"

Bert remained half standing for a moment, then stood up. "I think—"

"This offer is not for your employers. It is for you."

Bert stared at her. He opened his mouth to speak, then suddenly sat down. "I offer no promises at the present time."

"And I ask none. But I would like you to come down to our place of business. Experience for yourself what we do, see why we are better than what your employers have to offer. Then, if you are impressed, we will... make promises."

Shiela smiled.

A long, long moment while Bert studied Shiela. Another long moment while he gazed at Lucas.

"I am not looking for other employment," he said. But he didn't stand up.

"We weren't looking for a partner. In fact, all we can offer is shares. Do you get paid a salary? Is it based on performance? Some other method of recompense? Let's talk turkey, Bert. Anybody who isn't looking to better his situation is a fool. You don't impress me as a fool. Now I am offering you secrets which I have denied your employer. Yet if I can't convince you of certain items, you can tell your employers. Nothing for us, but everything for you. If you're not chicken."

She grinned at the last sentence, and it was obvious she was't playing the 'you're afraid' game with him. She was just playing with him.

"I don't think you know what you're getting into," he said with a broad smile of his own.

"It's up to you to surprise me."

Again, a long moment, and it was obvious that that was all Shiela had to offer.

Lucas, watching, wondered what was going to happen. Even though he preferred women, he could tell that Shiela was impressed by Bert. He wondered if she wanted Bert.

"Very well."

Shiela smiled, "One moment."

She stood up and went to the computer. She tapped in a series of commands. The doors were bolted, which Bert noted with sharp hearing. The brick wall in garage rose. The lights in the basement went on.

Shiela turned to Lucas. "If you could take Bert to our dungeon and show him around. I'll only be a moment."

Lucas took Bert's hand. It was soft, yet there was a gentle strength to his hand that said much. There was iron underneath those gentle muscles.

Shiela headed up stairs.

Lucas took Bert through the kitchen and into the garage. Shiela had opened the small room used as a staging area to the dungeon door and Lucas was surprised. This was really revealing all their little secrets.

Bert hesitated, and Lucas let go of his hand and watched while he inspected the little room.

There were no doors but the one. But the floor, when the lights would go out and the floor would rotate and anybody inside would lose all sense of direction. They would think that the little room would open on the back yard, or on the garage again. This would confuse anybody trying to fulfill a search warrant. They wouldn't know there even was a basement, the blueprints at building and planning at city hall had been replaced.

Bert turned and looked at the dungeon door. Iron with rivets and a small door at eye level.

He looked at Lucas and Lucas shrugged and indicated he should open the door.

They walked down stairs that were made of cinder blocks to a floor that was rough cement.

The basement, or dungeon, stretched half the width of the house and the full length. It was 1500 square feet, and it contained chains on the walls, furniture like a rack, a St. Andrew's Cross, benches for various uses, and so on.

At places around the dungeon were collections of whips, paddles, belts, feathers.

Inside drawers were vibrators, dildos, plugs, everything that a dominatrix, or a submissive, could want.

"My, my," murmured Bert. "You really have outdone yourselves."

"Does your places of business...are they as well fixed?"

"Not even. Compared to you they are cave people. Oh, they try hard, but...my employers are more concerned with money, not with the quality of the services."

"Quality is our service."

"Yes," and he appeared to be thinking.

Shiela descended the stairs, the powerful click, click, click of her heels drawing their attention.

She was wearing a black corset with a half bra, dark nylons and high heels, and she had put on full make up. Her hair was pony tailed on top and her lips were quirky smiling and red as glossed cherries.

Lucas, of course, was totally in love. His heart dropped out of his chest, he forgot to breath, and his heart swelled up.

But the affect on Bert was similar. He took in his breath at the sight of her swelling breasts, at the way her stiff nipples jutted out.

"My," he said, and that was all.

"Go get dressed Lucas. I'll get started with Bert."

Lucas headed upstairs. As he ascended to the ground floor he glanced at Shiela. She was standing face to face with Bert, and Bert was just staring.

Then Lucas was racing through the house and upstairs.

Bert looked to Shiela with an impassive face. He was mostly curious. He couldn't imagine anything this woman could do that would change his mind.

Shiela smiled, but it was a rigid smile, two hairs short of being a sneer.

"Have a seat," Shiela indicated the rack. It was obvious she wanted him not to just sit, but to allow himself to be restrained on it.

Bert took off his jacket loosened his tie, and lay on the rack. "Face up or down?" he inquired politely.

"Face up to start," responded Shiela. "And, before we get started, have you had experience with dungeons and dominatrices?"

"I have," he answered, laying on his back and raising his arms over his head.

Shiela fastened leather straps over his wrists, over his ankles, then stretched him. Not tight, just slightly uncomfortable.

She went to a cabinet and took out a razor knife. She sat down next to him and began to cut his clothes off.

Bert lay silently, watching.

"You know, I always wonder about flight 93. A couple of scrawny, probably wiry, Arabs, armed only with these," she held up the knife, then went back to slicing his trousers off.

"How much damage they must have done to the people trying to regain control of the plane. The cuts wouldn't have been deep, but the blades wouldn't stick, would send sprays of blood into the air. The screaming, the rage, the crying."

She pulled pieces of material off him, sliding strips out of his restraints.

Bert said nothing. But he was blinking.

"Since you're experienced, and I mean in more than sexual torments, you will understand what I am about to say. The extra item that we provide is that we care. This is the real difference between ours and your house, and that is not something that can be taught. How do you teach somebody how to care?"

She cut his underwear off, making sure to let him feel one of her fingernails. The nail felt like she was slicing his skin, and his pupils were dilating.

His penis was nicely sized. A bit bigger than average, but nothing that would cause pain in an inexperienced girl.

"Now, let's discuss what you do for your present employers. I'm fairly knowledgable about such matters, and you're not just a deal maker, you're an enforcer. You can correct me if I'm wrong, but we both know the truth here."

Bert said nothing. The feel of her finger 'slicing' along his skin was unnerving, though he did his best to not show it.

"So what are your next steps should I refuse your generous offer?"

She spoke as if she hadn't already said no. It was just a way of messing with his mind.

He didn't answer.

She didn't care.

He was naked now, fully erect, and Lucas came down the stairs and approached silently. Lucas was wearing heels, nylons, corset, and make up. His boobs were overflowing, jiggling just from him breathing. As he sat Bert turned his head and noted the lack of sex organs.

Lucas was sewed back between his legs, his mons looked like a pussy, but without the slit. The effect on Bert was to make him draw in his breath.

Lucas, in his eyes, was exotic.

Shiela didn't look at Lucas, and he wisely just pulled up a chair and watched.

"My next question would be as to how we could improve our security features. I know that you have already figured out what we've done, so what else can we do?"

Surprisingly, Bert answered. "Buy a gun. Lots of guns."

"Nonsense. We hardly need to risk a gunfight in suburbia."

"It won't be a gunfight. It will be an assassination."

"Yes, I suppose you're right."

Shiela sat on him. Right on his penis, slipped right over him, folded her arms on his chest and stared into his eyes. "I like you. Why don't you buy a gun and work for us. You could protect us, guard us against assassination, and if things progress, you could strike back for us. Hopefully before they strike first."

Bert was breathing hard. God, did he love the feel of her pussy.

"So we pay you in stocks, you become a working partner of sorts, we expand, you no longer work for peanuts."

"They pay me well."

"Not as good as stock options."

"Are you planning to go public?"

It was a joke, but not quite. His mind was getting seriously fucked, along with his dick, and he was trying to make a joke.

She didn't take it like a joke. She rose up, slid off him, grabbed the box cutter in one hand, his weenie in the other, and held the tip of the razor blade to his penis head.

"If I took off this it would decrease 90% of your penile sensation. And you'd be an inch shorter. Do you really want to make jokes with me?"

He swallowed, but that was all, then shook his head slightly.

She put down the box cutter and began turning him over. He was held taut, but the wrist restraints and the leg restraints were crossed, so she managed to simply flip him over.

And plug him.

"Gah!" he said.

But it wasn't bad. She took her time, greased him well, wiggled it gently, and by the time she was done, and he was officially plugged, he was gasping.

What he didn't know was that it was a pear of anguish.

A pear of anguish is an insidious, little device. The working end of a but plug can be expanded. Simply opened up. Once in, never out.

Shiela lay on him, let him feel her breasts flat on his back. She whispered into his ear, "I can break the base off this little device. It would be stuck in you big time. You'd need a doctor to operate, to actually open your anus with his surgical steel and remove it. Should I break it off?"

"Do what you want," he whispered.

She got off him, knelt by the side of the rack and hooked a suction tube to his penis. She fondled his balls briefly, then laid back down on him.

He was breathing heavily now, and it was obvious that he was going places he had never been before.

"You...you..."

Shiela was holding a remote and she clicked the switch.

She could feel the suction start up on the other side of his body. The little tube went up and down on his penis, slithering, sliding, letting him feel wonderful, and deprived, all at the same time.

"It won't let you cum. I won't let you cum. I want you in a bargaining frame of mind."

"I...I..."

His butt started to go up and down. He was already trying to contribute to the 'humping' action under the rack.

She kissed his neck, she nibbled on his ear.

She reached down and wiggled the pear of anguish, which caused him to give his first moan. It just erupted out of him, a palpable desire that could not be quelled...except by a squirt.

But if he squirted, and the torment went on, then it would become real torture.

She whispered in his ear.

Sitting to the side, Lucas couldn't hear what she was saying, but he had listened to Shiela's whispers himself, and he knew about them.

I love you. Give up. We're not stopping until you do.

But now her whispers were taking on new dimensions, soul shattering dimensions, for Shiela knew what kind of a person Bert was.

Bert was bad. He made deals, and if he couldn't, then he hurt them. hurt them bad.

Assassinated them.

Bert was the real deal.

But he had agreed to the dungeon, so there was a weakness. He wanted something. And what does everybody want?

Surprisingly, the answer is not sex. Though that is a close second. A close second that can, on occasion, overwhelm the mind, the soul, and even the desire for the first desire.

The first desire, as corny and unrealistic as it might sound, was love.

Everybody wants love. Love with sex, sex with love, but love.

Even when they just go out and buy sex, underneath that desire is the real thing. Love.

Shiela whispered of love, and Bert's mother, and his crimes, and how he was losing love by trying to replace it with his desires to make people submit to violence.

"It's not violence that is the answer," her voice slid into his ear canal. "Violence is just the make believe sex you have replaced love with."

And there were questions. How much do you make, who have you hurt and how, how can we improve security, what are your next steps should I refuse you?

Refuse you, bring this to an end and kick you out, stop my love of you.

After an hour Bert was talking a bit. Not a lot, but a bit.

Not because of the torture, but because if he unburdened himself, if he confessed, he would, at last, be open for love.

Shiela took out the pear of anguish, gave his butthole time to recover, and sat to one side and sipped a Coke. Her head was close to Lucas's, and she explained what she was doing.

"It's going to take a while," she said. "But he wants a better life."

"How do you know?"

"Because everybody wants a better life."

Back to the rack.

She wheeled a machine over. It was a motorized dildo, and she set it to work.

Now he wasn't feeling just the pain, and the sexual sensation of being opened up. Now he was feeling the motion, the in and out, the action of sex, as his mind broke down and began to consider what Shiela was saying.

"Work for us. On your days off I will put you on the rack, or one of the other incredible pieces of furniture that we have. I will leave you there all day. At last you can make up for all the bad things you have done. At last you can be honest, and maybe you can even deserve love. Would you like to deserve love? I want to love you, but you stop me. You won't even tell me how to protect myself. You won't pick up a gun and protect me. How can I love you when you refuse me like that?"

He still hadn't cum, and Shiela was careful not to let the pistoning dildo rub against his prostate. She kept it angled so the prostate wouldn't let his juices flow.

Three hours in. She had Lucas sit on him. Give his ass to the now groaning Bert.

Bert, quite honestly, didn't know if he was in a pussy or an ass, and certainly didn't care. His senses were rapidly leaving him, and that seem to bother him at all.

Lucas, interestingly enough, was able to treat Bert's dick like a dildo, to just use it and have a good time. That was sort of enlightening.

Five hours of non cumming, sexually stimulating, pleasurable pain and painful pleasure.

Shiela wasn't tired, she was unleashed.

Always she was circumspect with clients. She watched their limits, timed their enlightenments. But now she was ignoring everything, going for broke, taking Bert places where men rarely went.

Seven hours, and Bert was now begging. He wanted to cum, and he was answering questions.

Make a tunnel for secret access to the dungeon. He was being paid fifty thousand a year, which wasn't really as good as he pretended. He gave the locations of his employer's houses. He talked about the ladies they had working for them, some of whom would certainly be willing to come over to Shiela.

And so on.

Nine hours, and he was silent. This was far beyond any person Shiela had ever taken. But she wasn't going to stop.

How much sex can a human being take? How far can they be stimulated until the mind stops functioning and becomes a puddle of pudding, accepting everything, rejecting nothing, and...changes?

Lucas cooked a dinner of mush.

Shiela ate, and spoon fed Bert. She sat on his penis, still careful not to let him cum, and gently placed spoonfuls of mush into his sobbing mouth.

Lucas watched, and was almost in shock. Never had he seen a man so thoroughly taken apart. He was watching the most complete metamorphosis he could ever imagine.

At fifteen hours Bert asked if he cold go to work for Shiela.

"Of course," she replied. She unbuckled him. She helped him up, and walked up him upstairs. She took him to the guest bedroom and put him to bed.

She sat with him as he lay there, staring at her, in love, and wondering what was going to happen to him.

"We only have female clothes in this house, you can wear those and we can special order you some male clothes."

He mumbled an okay, unable to take his eyes off her.

"Now go to sleep. Please don't masturbate. I'll take care of you when you awake." She kissed him, rubbed his weenie for a long minute, then turned off the lights and closed the door.

Lucas was standing outside and listening. He heard a deep, deep sigh, the rustle of sheets, then nothing.

Shiela took Lucas's hand and led him down to the kitchen.

"Steak, honey. I need protein, and I'm way too tired to cook anything."

Lucas brought her a drink, and she sat at the table and nursed it. She was thoughtful, in her own world, and very, very tired.

"That takes something out of you," she murmured as the smell of cooking steaks filled the kitchen.

"Not to be cynical," said Lucas, "but will he stay, uh…converted?"

"Should. But maybe not. I think he will, though. Men need love."

Lucas nodded, then softly said, "Love on the end of a knife."

Shiela smiled. "The best kind."

Lucas brought steaks to the table and they ate.

Now Shiela was totally out of it. She was fed, she would have strength on the morrow, she wouldn't be wasted, but now she needed deep sleep.

Lucas helped her up and, like she had walked Bert upstairs, he walked her.

Shiela sighed, was unbalanced, but there was a subtle joy to her that Lucas couldn't help but note.

He took her into their bedroom, helped her undress. Undid her ponytail, which had been tight for almost 16 hours.

She shook her hair out gratefully.

He put cold cream on her face and gently wiped her make up off.

"Thank you, honey," she said as he helped her into bed.

He turned off the lights and closed the door.

He listened for a moment outside the door and heard the same rustle of sheets, the same deep, soul felt sigh, then…nothing.

She stopped by the door to the guest room and listened to Bert. He was breathing deeply and rhythmically and giving little snores.

Then Lucas went down to the basement. He sat on the rack and just sat. He looked around, and imagined what Bert must have seen, what he had felt.

He laid down, duplicating Bert's positions. He gripped the ropes with his hands, hooked his feet in the straps, and pulled tight.

Lucas had met people like Bert. He didn't understand them like Shiela did, but he understood enough.

They bullied in school.

They were first in line and took the biggest portions.

They laughed at people as they shoved them out of the way.

But Lucas thought that maybe Bert had changed.

In his experience people changed very little, especially the ones who were rigid in their minds and personalities.

But Bert, he thought, had changed.

So now they were three. Three people to administer a business that had grown so fast in such a short time that it was actually unnerving.

He and Shiela had talked about that. About how to hire people. About how to make a bigger facility when the demand reached higher levels.

And he thought about his father.

Grant. A big time lawyer who was currently making some kind of world class contracts in China.

What would his father think?

He had fucked his father's wife. They had used his bank account freely to build their business.

Their sex business.

Whoever came up with the phrase 'sex sells' really knew what they were talking about.

His father was due home in less than two weeks.

What would he do?

What would they do?

They would move the business; they would have to have another home for their undertaking.

Would his father be pissed?

Well, the actual question would be how much would his father be pissed.

Enough to disown him? Enough to divorce his wife?

Lucas got off the rack and stood up. With a final look around the room he headed upstairs where he poured a final drink for the night. A little rum and Coke. A little zonker to help put him to sleep.

He stood by the kitchen window and looked out at the neighborhood.

What would the neighbors think? He and Shiela had been so low key the neighbors had no idea what was going on under their very noses.

Would there be lawsuits? Lots of publicity?

Yes, probably lots of publicity. People were aghast at Jeffrey Epstein's Island, they would never go there, but they sure wanted to hear about it.

And what were he and Shiela doing but creating their own suburban version of Epstein's Island.

Then, his final serious thought for the night: what would Bert's boss do?

They had tried the police and failed. They had sent their 'enforcer' over, and he had failed.

And who were his bosses?

Were they just high end politicians?

Or were they real crooks?

Lucas snorted a laugh as he thought this. Is there any real difference between a high end politician and a criminal?

So thinking, he finished his drink, washed his glass out and placed it in the dish drainer next to the sink. Then he walked upstairs where he slipped quietly into bed next to Shiela and closed his eyes.

Part Two

Bert was a changed man; he was in love.

Lucas observed this from the first day after Bert's conversion. The way Bert stared after Shiela. The way his now puppy dog eyes glowed at the sight of her.

And Lucas knew this because he had gone through this state of mind. Was currently in this state of mind.

To live for the kind stroke of a hand, the brush of the lips against his cheek, the smile…it gave purpose to life.

Of course, there were differences between Lucas and Bert.

Lucas had been a spoiled brat. A nerd with no experience.

Bert was not a spoiled brat, but he was a bully of immense proportions.

Now his whole persona had been altered, redirected.

That first morning after they all sat down for breakfast, and there was a glee in the air.

"What can I do for you?" Bert didn't ask about shares, or sex, or even love. He just wanted to know what he could do.

"Get us some guns. Increase security. Dig a tunnel."

"Okay."

Just a smile and an acknowledgement. The power of the dominatrix was absolute.

Their day off over, Shiela and Lucas began preparing for that night's tour of the dungeon. They answered emails, they ran checks on people, they discussed who they would invite, and who should be on a waiting list.

Meanwhile, Bert began work on an escape plan.

"You don't understand," he told Shiela at breakfast. "My bosses are above the politicians. They are criminals."

Innocent Lucas asked, "But how can that be?"

"It's simple, explained Bert. Politicians deal in votes. Criminals deal in bullets. Which one do you think will win a fight?

There followed a long talk about what kind of criminals used guns, and which kind used pens.

While Lucas had questions, Shiela merely smiled and listened. She already knew the arguments, and that was why she had enlisted Bert in their cause.

In the far corner of the basement was a small room that looked like it had been used for coal. It turned out that it had, and that the chute had been covered up.

Bert uncovered the chute, expanded it, and made a long ditch along the side of the yard. He dug it behind some bushes, and when it was deep enough he laid sheets of metal over the ditch, tossed in dirt, and started a lawn.

Shiela and Lucas was amazed at how much one man could do when he was inspired.

"You better reward him with a cum," whispered Lucas in an aside to Shiela.

"Nah," she said with a grin.

Well, Shiela knew best. A horny man is an industrious man.

Past the patio and the pool was a slight rise, then a fence, and beyond the fence was a house for sale.

Bert bought it and took the tunnel all the way to the basement of that house.

Lucas picked up a couple and three men. He offered them drinks on the way back to the house, and Bert, dressed in his best, made the libations.

"Are you a couple?" asked one of the men.

Bert and Lucas smiled at each other.

"No."

"Oh, I thought…" and the man trailed off, but he had his eyes on Lucas. Shiela had been right, men were fascinated by trannies.

They all entered the house and the lockdown was enacted. Bolts were shot on the doors, the rotating room at the entrance to the dungeon was opened, and the thick, brick wall that covered the entrance to the dungeon was raised.

Paperwork was completed, more drinks were served, and the party was taken out to the garage.

Everybody pushed into the little room outside the entrance to the dungeon. The walls turned, the floor turned, and everybody expected to go out the door at the back of the garage.

Instead, they were confronted by the iron door.

Lucas opened the door and smiled as everybody trudged down past him.

Once in the basement of the men was chained to the wall. He grinned and joked, and was not truly prepared for what was about to happen.

One was put on the rack, one on the St. Andrew's Cross, and one on the padded horse.

The woman was given a dominatrix outfit. She was there to observe, to learn the proper way to administer love to her husband.

Then began one of the wildest nights Lucas had ever experienced.

He, Shiela and the woman, whose name was Sandy, used box knives to cut off clothes,

Shiela showed the woman how to wield the knife, how to stretch the clothes and slice them so she could pull them off the men.

There were murmurs from the men, but also a sober attitude. Those knives were sharp. And it didn't help when Shiela said, "Don't worry if you accidentally cut somebody. They only bleed for a while.

A man named Tom cleared his throat and said, "I think I've changed my mind."

"Of course you have," said Shiela, putting a penis gag in his mouth.

"MPHOOPHMMM!"

Shiela kneed him gently in the groin. Not enough to hurt, but enough to make the man turn white and shut up.

Shiela turned to Lucas, "Watch him. If he starts to puke get the gag out of his mouth.

The man stared at Lucas. He was pale and looked sickly, but he didn't throw up.

Shiela went around the room. She placed a dildo machine at the heinie of Jeremy, who was on the padded horse.. She turned on the dildo machine and everybody watched as Jeremy's eyes opened.

"Shock and delight," whispered Shiela to Sandy. "You need to shock them with delight."

Sandy's husband was moaning loudly, and wiggling his butt back at the dildo machine. He could feel the slick penis shafting him, opening him up, turning his world upside down.

She put a machine operated fleshlight on Jimmy, who was tied to the St. Andrew's cross.

She showed Sandy how to attach milking equipment to penises or nipples.

Soon the basement was a pit of grunting, straining, struggling men. Men exuding the desire to squirt, but unable, and that's when the real fun began.

There were four men and a girl as customers. Shiela and Lucas, with the help of the girl who was there to learn, went from man to man.

Lucas learned the fine points of wiggling butt plugs. He kissed lips, nuzzled necks, wiggled plugs, and stroked gently.

He made sure nobody came.

Shiela helped Sandy into a strap on and the two women went from man to man, Shiela screwing first, lecturing, teaching the fine points. Sandy proved to be an excellent student.

After a couple of hours the men were exhausted. They sagged from their chains or straps, gasped for breath, and felt the electric sensation of expanded assholes.

The girls sat on a spare padded bench and discussed techniques.

The men listened, and were stunned by how they had been changed.

But that's men for you. They always think they're so big and brave, then the fun starts, and they find out the truth.

Women can easily withstand more pain than men, and they know it, so they had to be gentle. But being gentle was a blessing, because the men found it hard to fight loving pain. It was easy to fight hard pain, the struggle against the whips and spankings.

But how do you fight against the loving touch? The pain administered with love and care?

And so the days went.

Bert finished the tunnel and began another one, one that would take a while to complete, but would lead away from both houses.

He set up a second secret server in the back house. He magnetized the house, which was a Godsend, once Shiela thought about it.

And he hired girls.

He knew every girl that worked for his former bosses. He had used just about every girl that worked for his bosses, and they all liked him.

Funny how a fellow with such violent potential could make women love him, and yet fall so totally, head over heels in love with Shiela.

But that's the way it is sometimes. A man's greatness strength becomes his greatest weakness.

But for all his preparations the world was about to fall in.

The way the world works is people work, then give their money to politicians. Or, the politicians reach in and take it, barely leaving enough for the citizen to live.

If a person can't pay enough the politician sics the muscle on them. On a national level this is the IRS, augmented by CIA, Homeland security, FBI, or whatever organization is deemed most powerful and able to take the citizen's money, property, etc.

On a local level this is usually the police or the sheriff or whatever police force is deemed appropriate to run people out of their homes, arrest them, etc.

The problem in this case was the politicians had tried the police first, and failed. So they had turned to their superiors, the crime bosses who got them elected, bought them off, etc., who sent in Bert.

But Bert had failed, and that meant the next level of enforcement, but since the police had already been tried, that meant actual criminals. Thugs. People with guns.

If people refuse to pay for protection, normally called taxes, the government will take them to court.

When the government can't take people to court they simply move in and destroy them.

So that was what was going to happen to Shiela and Lucas. Bert expected this. He didn't, however, expect the level of escalation that was about to happen.

He thought a couple of thugs would be sent over. Maybe some rocks through the front window, some tires slashed, that sort of thing.

Friday night was the busiest night of the week. That was the end of the work week, and people were prone to pursuing their favorite hobby, such as getting their ass spanked, being reamed out by a dildo made of ginger root, or just getting royally fucked by an extra big penis.

One woman kept asking her husband, "Why are we doing this? What are we doing here?" She did this all the way in the limo ride, then grinned when she entered the living room. She was looking forward to getting some intense instruction concerning the right way to handle her husband.

Paperwork was taken care of, drinks were served, everybody was happy and cheerful.

The security features were enacted. Bolts shot,

While there was usually a heavy preponderance of men, on this night it was equal. Six men and six women.

The group was divided, three men and three women in the front house, and three men and three women were taken to the back house.

The six going to the house behind Shiela's loved the tunnel. It was a great adventure. They all giggled and played grab ass and their horniness was enhanced by the cloak and dagger stuff.

Lucas was in the back house, and this was his first time of being in sole control of the festivities.

Shiela was in the front house, each of them had a girl brought in by Bert to train.

Everything started out nicely. The customers were strapped to tables and crosses and benches, or simply chained to the walls.

Clothes were cut off wholesale. Strips of trousers and skirts accumulated on the floors. Buttons popped. Zippers and belts were ripped apart and boners were sprang and pussies were revealed.

Then the real fun started.

In the front house Shiela showed her assistant, a girl named Cindy, the right way to drain a man, stopping, of course, before any sizable amount of semen was produced.

In the rear house Lucas demonstrated how to tease a man with boobs and the promise of a lowering pussy. Of course, since Lucas didn't have a pussy, he would show to a point, then have his assistant, a girl named Francie, take over.

Unless, of course, he felt the wonderful anal itch that had become his life.

"That's it, Francie. Take just the head. Now wiggle a bit, tease that head. How you doing, Tom?"

The man under Francie tried to talk, but his speech was failing him.

In the front house Shiela carved a ginger root in front of Max, who was tied to the St. Andrew's cross. He watched the way the sharp knife scalloped the root, he gulped as he anticipated the burning sensation he was about to endure.

Shiela handed the ginger root to Cindy. "Now, put it in like I showed you."

Around the basement men were moaning, trapped on benches or by chains, their manhood imprisoned and abused by fleshlights with tiger balm lubrication, or their assholes savaged by dildos of varying sizes and shapes.

Max's feet were spread by the cross and Cindy worked the root into his nethers, then she straightened up and pressed her large boobs against him, kissed his ear and his neck, and worked the root further and further into the man.

Max tried not to say anything, but that was impossible. The burning sensation shot through him, made his penis stand up all the harder.

"A little more in and out, Cindy. Max is not fragile. He can take it."

"I can't," burbled Max, tears running down his cheeks. But his cock was dripping uncontrollably.

"Sure you can. Slap his balls, but be careful, look at the mess he is making."

Drip splat. Drip splat. The floor was turning slickery under his faucet cock.

In the back house was discussing how many fingers to use.

"Men are babies," Lucas explained to Francie. It takes a while to open them up. Women are voracious, however. Watch this." Lucas inserted his fingers slowly, jabbed a few times, reamed, and then slipped his fist into one of the women.

The woman, name of Lucy, moaned and spread her legs wider.

Lucas took his hand out and replaced it with a huge bulbous headed penis. "This will hold Lucy for a while, now watch what happens when I try the same thing to her husband."

Lucas placed one finger in the man's rectum, then two. He reamed and jabbed, then three. The man, Tom, was now purple faced, and he was about at his limit.

"You see? Now Tom can take it all, but you need to spend some time for that to happen. Here, put that dildo in him and leave it."

Francine pushed a long dildo with bumps along the side in Tom, and they moved on to the next customer.

And so it went, Shiela and Lucas teaching, teaching both the two girls they had enlisted for the enterprise, and the several women who had expressed a desire to learn how to rule their husbands.

Upstairs at the front house Bert was checking the systems. Being on the giving end of 'punishments' for competition, he had developed a sixth sense, and right then his sixth sense was lighting up.

He had set up cameras to watch the streets leading to the houses, but they weren't showing anything.

But how long would it take for a couple of cars of thugs to zoom down the street, pile out and pound the door down?

Even with the bolts, the doors wouldn't last more than a minute or two. Eventually he would replace the jams with metal, then the bolts would hold long enough for everybody to scoot.

But…why was his internal 'radar' blinking so furiously?

He called a colleague of his, but there was no answer.

Finally, feeling a bit of frustration, he typed in the city name and 'live police scanner.'

He heard the endless chatter, and frowned. There wasn't enough endless chatter. On a Friday night the police radio should be going crazy. Fights and drag races, domesticate disputes and loud music. Accidents and drunks and…it was calm.

Yet he knew it wasn't calm. It was impossible for it to be calm on a Friday night.

He knew there were other channels, but he didn't know how to access them, he was looking across the net for a method of finding other police channels when the cars started roaring up the street.

He didn't hesitate, he only had a few minutes. If that.

He slapped a key and the alarm bell went off. In both houses a loud clanging was heard.

Shiela knew what it was immediately.

"Get everybody loose."

In the back house Lucas was startled, and puzzled, then figured it out. "Pull the dildos and plugs out, let everybody loose."

On the computer Bert saw the cars coming down the street the back house was located on.

Damn! They knew about the back house, and the back house was not fully secure! The thugs would break through the front door like it was balsa wood!

He poked the number for Lucas's cell.

Lucas answered within a second. Around him Francie was letting people out of their restraints. Everybody was wondering what was going on, talking and shouting and looking around.

"Lucas! Get back to the house. Use the tunnel!"

Lucas acknowledged, and started pushing people towards the tunnel. Within a minute everybody was rushing down the tunnel. Some were worried and wondered what was going on. Some were giggling at this new adventure.

The sound of the doors upstairs reached Lucas's ears just as he pulled the door shut to the tunnel.

Customers rushed out of the tunnel into the dungeon basement of the front house, and now there was a problem None of them had any clothes on.

The most clothes anybody wore were the dominatrix outfits worn by Shiela and Lucas, and the suit worn by Bert.

Everybody gathered in the front house basement and chattered. They were concerned, but not alarmed. To them this was all part of the 'dungeon tour.' A new gimmick thought up by Shiela and Lucas. Imagine! running around naked, boobs and dicks bouncing, what fun!

Shiela headed up the stairs and everybody started following them.

Bert had backed up to the stairway that led upstairs. He had a gun in each hand. The guns were Glocks with 20 round magazines. He had a lot of firepower.

Shiela rushed into the kitchen and people started crowding into the kitchen behind her.

Somebody was looking through the kitchen window and shouting, but whatever was said was lost in the racket created by the dozen customers shouting back and forth in glee.

"Stay back!" shouted Bert.

BANG! The front door shivered.

BANG! Shiela say splinters coming out of the jam, and the locations where the bolts were started to bulge outward.

"What's going on?" screamed Shiela.

"We're getting raided!"

BANG!

"No! Get back in the dungeon. I've called the....." his voice couldn't be heard for the banging on the front door and the screams of the happy customers.

BANG!

Shiela turned and motioned everybody back, but now she was being pushed by the people behind her, and she fell into the living room.

BANG! The door flew inward. It hung by one hinge, and it barely missed Shiela's head.

BANG! BANG BANG! These weren't the sound of a battering ram striking the front door, these were the sound of Bert's Glocks firing rapidly.

Shouts! Screams! BANG! BANG BANG! Whoever was outside returned fire.

BANG! BANG BANG! Bert moved up the stairs, making a moving target that the thugs outside couldn't seem to hit.

BANG! BANG BANG!

People falling over Shiela in the front room, screaming and crying as they tried to get away.

BANG! BANG BANG!

BANG! BANG BANG!

BANG! BANG BANG!

Then it was silent.

Deathly silent.

Then the moans started.

"Oh! I'm hit."

"I've got blood on me!"

Bert was upstairs, kneeling, breathing hard. He had taken a bullet to the chest.

Outside were more moans. "Fucker shot me!"

"Somebody help me!"

Then the gangsters moved through the door.

More gangsters had found the tunnel and were now coming up the stairs from the dungeon.

People lay naked, bleeding, crying, and wondering what had happened.

They had been having so much fun! But now they were bleeding, and they didn't understand.

Slowly, the chaos began to recede.

Gangsters stood around if they weren't injured, collapsed on the floor or the couch if they were.

The room was a mess, between bullet holes in flesh and walls, shattered windows and busted doors, the house was virtually destroyed.

The sound of sirens intruded on the mess. The police, late as usual, were arriving, which didn't necessarily bode well for the customers.

More people raising their voices, asking for help. Wondering what happened. One voice even begged for his mother.

Shiela dragged herself out from under the mess of bodies. People laying on her had been shot, but that had protected her.

Lucas picked his way over the carnage and hugged Shiela and helped her get free.

"Help the people," Shiela whispered.

Lucas started unentangling victims. He did his own sort of triage, moving gunshot victims to an area in front of the fireplace, and enlisted those not injured to help him.

Slowly, order was appearing, then the police appeared, and once again chaos was installed.

"Hands up! Drop your guns!" Orders were screamed, and gangsters slipped pistols under the cushions of chairs and couches.

Bert was sitting against the wall, knowing that he was about to check out, and wishing he could have had more time to love Shiela.

The police shoved people around and destroyed the order Lucas had been creating.

For long minutes the police got in the way, then the people crying for help were heard and the police started actually doing something right.

Bandages appeared, tourniquets were tightened, even morphine was injected.

Then everything went silent. Not all at once, but like a wave spreading out from the front door.

The gangsters paled. The police turned and paled, the people, seeing the reactions of the gangsters and police, and where they were staring, turned their heads and looked at the front door.

A little figure stood in the doorway. She wore a cheongsam with portholes for her breasts. Breasts that were even bigger than Lucas's. She had a slit up the side of her dress showing the curvy flesh of stunning legs.

Dead silence, except for wounded moans, and even these seemed to fade in the appearance of the sexy, little woman in the doorway.

Then one of the gangsters blurted, "Boss!"

All of the gangsters shrunk back.

One of the cops said, "Oh, no." And all of the cops recognized the little woman. She was a leader of the city, head of the civic council, more powerful than the mayor.

Of course she looked quite a bit different now, but everybody recognized the little figure.

Shiela said, "Grant?"

Grant stepped into the room, and his face was inscrutable. He was no longer the dapper, older gent. He seemed to have lost years in his transition, and now he was a sexy, young appearing woman. Large breasts, soft lips, long hair, but still the powerful aura of the alpha dog of all alpha dogs.

"Pop?" wondered Lucas.

"What the holy, fucking hell has been going on!"

Several of the gangsters shat their pants right then.

Several of the clients smiled. At last, a face they recognized, even if he did seem a little pissed. Maybe they could get to the bottom of why they had been shot.

Epilogue

Grant sat on a chair and faced the room.

The injured were laying directly in front of him. Behind them the gangsters stood, looking very nervous. Behind them the police stood, and they were pretty unnerved, too.

EMTs had arrived and the injured were being attended to. The medics walked softly and said nothing. There was some serious shit going down. A gunfight between the police and the gangsters, and now everybody was looking down at the ground and worrying.

"Okay," said Grant. "You guys who have been shot. Do you want to be shot some more, or will you take a million dollars for your suffering, plus all medical bills to be paid by me."

Since the customers knew Grant, and since the choice wasn't a hard one, they all smiled and counted themselves lucky.

One of the clients, who had not been shot, said, "What about me? I wasn't shot, but do I get a million dollars?"

Grant turned to one of the gangsters. "Shoot him."

The gangster, who had retrieved his gun from the couch, shot the man in the shoulder.

"OW!"

"Okay. You get a million. Anybody else?"

That was an interesting moment, for several had not been shot, and now they had to make a decision.

"Okay, you naked people, clear on out."

The customers made their way to the door, or were transported by EMTs on stretchers. The gangster and police made way and even lent a hand.

Grant addressed the police. "What the fuck do you bozos mean shooting up one of my houses?"

The police all said they were sorry.

"That's okay. I'll pay you overtime and time and a half and even a bonus if you promise never to do it again. Anything else?"

"No, sir," said a sergeant, and all the cops headed for the shattered doorway.

Grant's face took on a more serious look, and now the gangsters were even more worried.

"Now then, who wants to explain why you guys are here."

All of the gangsters started talking over each other.

"Hold it! You, Jocko, what's up?"

"We got a call from the mayor. You wasn't around, so we figured...he made it sound important, and Bert, he went over to the other side, and—"

Grant held up his hand. "Where's Bert."

Everybody looked around, and Jocko muttered, "He conked out at the top of the stairs."

Grant frowned, and a couple of the gangsters flinched.

"Okay. I want you to take Bert and any other bodies out of here. Dispose of them in the regular manner. Jocko. Go shoot the mayor."

Jocko started for the door.

"But only shoot him a little, got it?"

"Yes, boss!" Jocko was glad to get out of there.

"Now then, the rest of you. I forgive you. Go to Bernie's Liquors and tell him to give you a case of scotch. Good scotch. Head out for the hide out and I don't want to see you for a week. Muggsie, is that enough booze?"

"Better make it two cases."

"Okay. Two cases, now get the fuck out of here before I remember that I'm mad."

The room cleared of gangsters in a jiffy.

Which left broken furniture, holes in the walls, the poor front door, and Shiela and Lucas.

Grant turned to them.

He eyed Shiela. "So you want to go into business for yourself."

"Honey, I didn't—"

Grant held up a hand. "You have my blessing. You will also remain married to me. I don't care who else you fuck, I seem to have misplaced my weenie, and that's no reason for you to lose out on sex. Just keep it on the quiet. Got it?"

Shiela looked demurely at the floor. "Yes, dear."

Then Grant turned his attention to Lucas. "My son," he smiled. "I assume you noticed that I have changed into a woman. I didn't really go to China, I went to Thailand, and...well, you can see."

"Yes, father."

Grant frowned. "Are you still an asshole?"

"No, sir. Shiela showed me the error of my ways."

Grant turned back to Shiela and nodded approvingly, then he stood up and approached Lucas.

Lucas stood up. He was nervous, but not scared.

Grant hugged his son, their breasts mashed together, then Grant stood back and held his son at arm's length.

"My son. The apple doesn't fall from the tree, does it?"

"No, sir."

And they hugged again.

END

A Note from the Author!

I hope you liked this little tale
Please take a moment to rate me five stars.
That helps support my writing,
and lets me know which direction I should take
for future books.

HAVE A HORNY DAY!

Grace

You can find Grace Mansfield titles at
https://gropperpress.wordpress.com

If a link doesn't work for Amazon
you can sometimes find a title
by searching 'The Title Grace Mansfield,'
or by going to the author's page on Amazon.

Go to Amazon:
The Castration
Chronicles!

Here are the first three chapters from…

I CHANGED MY HUSBAND INTO A WOMAN!

A delightful novel of total power exchange!

GRACE MANSFIELD

I Changed My Husband into a Woman!

PROLOGUE

My husband likes jokes. Bad jokes. And everybody hates his bad jokes. But he keeps doing them. Why does he keep doing them? Because his name is Roscoe Tannenbaum. That's right, 'that' Roscoe Tannenbaum. Hollywood producer, jet setter, man about town…joker.

My name is Sandy Tannenbaum. Wife to the big man. And, believe me, that is a mixed bag of benefits and curses.

On one hand, I get to go to all the parties, I am held up as an important woman, and, I don't mind saying, I am genetically blessed.

What? You thought Roscoe would pick a shlump for a wife?

No way. I won several beauty contests when I was younger, and I decided, then and there, that being beautiful was the way to get ahead in the world. So I dedicated myself to improving myself. I spend more time at gyms than the owners. And I spent a LOT of time and money getting facials and learning the latest methods for staying beautiful. And, I hate to say it, but I am a friend of botox, silicon, and a lot of other chemical and surgical enhancers.

No way I am going to turn into an old rag and get tossed out by my asshole husband.

I know, you wonder how I can call him an asshole, especially just for a few bad jokes. Well, read on, and when you have heard me out then maybe you'll understand how revenge can be sweet, and whether the punishment fits the crime.

Ready? Then let's rock!

CHAPTER ONE

The day it all came apart, the day my husband made a date for his comeuppance, started out typically. The night before had been late and wild. We had gone to a party, everybody got sloshed, harder drugs made their appearance, and we were the last dogs to be hung.

Well, at least Roscoe was.

I'm careful. I always have a drink, but usually I only sip, and then only until I can find a way to replace my whiskey with a Pepsi. This is just one of the ways that I preserve my appearance.

Roscoe, on the other hand, drank from every bottle, smoked from every joint, and took every pill. The amazing thing about this was that he was always the last one standing.

So last night he was in typical high spirits, literally, and when the wee hours hit I helped him to the car, pushed him into the back, then drove home.

Oddly, it was a relaxing time. Him absent from the world, the world wound down to the few people getting the really early start to work, and me enjoying the drive to our Beverly Hills mansion.

I waited for the gate to open, then drove up the long drive. I pulled the car up to the entrance, then set about getting Roscoe upstairs.

Tugging a body pretty near dead to the world out of a car is not easy. The body to be moved snorts and grunts, rolls and flings its arms and legs out, and is generally resistant to the idea of being transferred to a nice, comfy bed.

I struggled for several minutes, got him half out of the car, and thought about leaving him there.

If he had been all the way in the car I would have done it. He hates waking up to find himself in the back of the car, but the wages of sin, you know.

I thought about getting him all the way out and then just throwing a blanket over him, but that seemed a bit much.

So, sighing, I went into the house and knocked on Juanita's bedroom door.

"Juanita?"

A moment while I heard the squeak of bedsprings and the rustle of clothes being put on, then the door opened.

Juanita came over the border illegally, and we hired her. When the SHTF and people started looking around for illegals to deport, we realized that Juanita was worth her weight in gold, and we found a good lawyer to help her get legal.

"Si, senorita Sandy?"

"I'm sorry, I need help getting Roscoe upstairs."

Juanita smiled ruefully. "Senor Roscoe," and she shook her head. "Let me get the shoes on."

I waited, and within 20 seconds we were hurrying back out to the car.

"Senor Roscoe, he need take care of heemself."

"You're telling me."

We managed to get him out of the car, then, blessing of blessings, Roscoe woke half up.

"Hey! I'm being kidnapped by beautiful girls!" We supported him, and we walked him up to the front door.

He stumbled and rolled, but managed to stay on his feet.

"It's Juanita! Are you taking me to Mehico?"

That's my rotten, husband. The bad side of good is that he flirts with every woman in the world. Of course, he protests that he is just friendly, that that is the Hollywood way. But I always suspicion…but I never found any evidence. Lots of rumors, but rumors are cheap fare in Hollywood. It's how actors and actresses get famous, and to pay attention to loose lips is to sink rowboats.

So we walked/dragged my stumblebum, drunken man through the foyer, up the long, winding stairway, and down the hall to our bedroom.

"Hee getting heavier," Juanita puffed. She was a chunky girl, not in great shape, but I was in great shape, and I was puffing, too.

"Don't feed him so much," I grunted.

She giggled. "I just put plate out. He keep eating and eating."

We reached the bed and pushed him onto it. We had done this before, and we knew that a big push might get him all the way onto the bed. If we were lucky.

We were lucky, and Roscoe landed, rolled, and snored.

"Okay, Senorita Sandee?"

"Thank you, Juanita. Sorry to have disturbed your sleep."

Again, she giggled. "Thee more I do thees the bigger Senor Roscoe pay me at Christmas."

I shook my head ruefully. The good side of bad. Roscoe had more money than God after a tax return and he did like to share. He paid people who worked for him well, which was good, because they had to put up with his bad jokes.

"Get what you can, Juanita, and more power to you."

She giggled, she was a giggling girl, and left the room.

I took off his shoes, then his socks. Pew. He must have forgot to wash his feet. He was always in such a hurry, making deals, producing movies and TV series, that he sometimes passed right by personal hygiene.

When I complained he was abashed, but how could I blame him? He was in a hurry to make a billion dollars. Well, to be honest, a trillion. He often joked about being the first trillionaire on earth. It was a joke, but behind the joke was a serious hard charger.

I worked his body around and got his jacket off, then his shirt, then his undershirt. I pulled his pants down, he wasn't wearing underwear, and my hubbie was officially naked.

I stared at Roscoe. He was a handsome man. A few years and I was sure his hard living would catch up to him. But right now he was slender, well cut, and only a trace of the 'heaviness' that Juanita had observed could be seen. Of course his eyes were a bit puffy.

Sometimes, after a hard night of partying his eyes were so puffy that I had to put make up on them.

Oh, not mascara and eye shadow and all that, but a light foundation type of cream to disguise the shadows. He had to appear happy and healthy, and not drunk as a dog, if he was going to keep making those million dollar deals.

Though, to be honest, the bad side of my good, I often thought about making his eyes up the feminine way, and not letting him know. That would serve him right.

I stared at his manhood. It was big, and it just laid there, a sleeping slug. The good side of bad, when that slug engorged it was a monster. It filled my hand, and my pussy, and made me cry and moan and scratch his back.

But now, after a long night, I stood there and watched it sleep.

I was horny. I wanted a little pleasure. I had had a long night of flirting, it's what we do in Hollywood, with young stars and starlets, and my pussy itched. Hell, I was downright wet.

I leaned forward and placed my hand under the slug. I lifted it up, shook it. Damn, if it had woken up I would have jumped him, asleep or not.

But it was not to be.

So I took off my own clothes, put some blinders on so the sun wouldn't wake me, and crawled into bed. Within seconds I was snoring. Ladylike snores, of course. But snores, nevertheless.

And that was how the day began, the day that started the 'unravelment' of my dear husband. When we awoke things were going to get interesting, and even more interesting as the day progressed, and good things and bad were going to come to light, and the devil would get his due. My husband, the rich and fabulously wealthy power player known as Roscoe Tannenbaum, was about to get his just rewards.

CHAPTER TWO

I was tired, it was still earlier, and I was lazing, half in and half out, occupying the twilight zone of barely asleep but hearing bits and pieces of the world.

I heard Roscoe stir. He placed a hand on my hip. He pulled lightly. He wanted some.

But I felt like I had barely gotten to sleep, and it was his fault. No way I was going to rouse myself and do the good and happy in and out. "Go way," I grumped.

I heard him say something. A return grump, no doubt. Then I felt the bed rustle.

I was going back to full sleep. I needed it. It was beauty sleep, after all, and I was addicted to being beautiful.

The bed shook a little bit more. I was half dreaming now, and I imagined myself in an earthquake, running down the street, the street shaking and buildings falling down. I was carrying something…a bundle, like groceries, like…like…A BABY?

I was carrying a baby in my dream running away from an earthquake, and suddenly somebody stepped out and shot me in the back. I lurched forward and found myself lying asprawl on my bed, blood dripping down my back, blood…BLOOD!

I snapped fully awake then, and I knew what had happened.

Roscoe rolled out of bed and padded towards the bathroom. After a night of carousing he was chipper and bright. "Good morning, love!" And he laughed.

I sat up and felt my back. Yuck! He had squirted on me! All over my hair! My gown! Mother fucker!

"You son of a bitch!" I yelled after him.

He laughed merrily. "Never say no to The Man!"

I climbed out of bed and staggered into the bathroom. I was not like him, I was not chipper after a night of carousing.

I stepped into his roaring shower and mumbled, "Wash my back, you son of a bitch."

So he did. And he worked shampoo into my hair and washed that, too. And then he soaped my goddamn breasts.

Ah, gad! I leaned against the tiles. The man was hornier than a goat playing a slide trombone. I felt my nipples perk up, I felt the electricity head towards my groin, and I knew that son of a bitch was going to get his way. He was going to get to climb into my cockpit and fly. After squirting his seed all over me!

"You just came," I complained.

"So? Maybe I can cum again. And if I can't, at least I can say I've been to see God this morning."

"Jesus," I moaned. I was wet. Of course I was wet. I was in the shower. But I was wet down there, with my own juices.

"I'll see him, too, my sweet, little pussy pie."

"You are so fucking..." I didn't finish as I was busy latching on to his lips, sucking his tongue like I was going to eat it.

"Oh, baby," he moaned.

Then I was down on my knees. Could he cum twice? It had happened before. Maybe, if I...then I got an evil idea.

I sucked and I sucked. I rolled his balls in my hands. Then I leaned back and spread my legs and he moved into me. He thrust his hips forward and slid his monster half into my vagina.

"Ahhh," he groaned. It was an awkward position, and he could only get halfway into me. He tried and tried, lurching and tilting his hips, but I kept a careful position and all he could do was get the head and an inch or two into me.

"Come on, baby," he was pleading, but I don't think he really knew how I was controlling the situation.

He was in, the head was in paradise, but he couldn't get in far enough to do the old in and out. He just kept pushing and pushing, his face turning all red, and just when it looked like he was going to pop, I tilted my hips away and pushed his chest.

"Wha—" he looked confused.

"Thanks, lover, got to go." I stepped out of the shower.

Oh, he roared. "You...you...BITCH!"

But I was laughing, and I knew he would laugh when he thought about it. That's the good side of his bad, he didn't mind a joke being played on him.

Of course, my joke wasn't over.

In the bedroom I laid on the bed, legs spread, and played with myself. I placed a dildo into my pussy and played the clitoris with a vibrator. A few minutes passed and he stepped out of the bathroom...just as I let loose.

"AHHHH!" My hips jerked and my eyes were glazed, but I could see his jaw drop.

I surged and moaned and bucked. I actually sprayed a bit of fluid.

Through my half slitted eyes I could see him standing so forlorn, his pecker standing up like a pirate about to board, all eager and dripping.

Then, when the spasms faded and I was left panting and loose and spread out like a flower that had been trampled, I said, "You can squirt all over my hair anytime you want, big boy."

A rueful grin flitted across his face—I told you he liked a good joke —and he said, "I should have known better."

"Ah, but you didn't," I rolled out of bed and came to him. I kissed him soundly, stroked his mighty machine, then pushed him away. "See you tonight, lover. Maybe."

He laughed.

Then we both got dressed and began our days. Him making million dollar deals, and me…I had to look beautiful. It was my job, after all.

While he put the screws to money men, and hired and fired camera crews and make up artists and went over scripts with producers, I went to the gym.

While he snarled and bellowed, and ended up with a good deal for all involved, I went spinning, and rode twenty miles without moving an inch.

While he went to a fancy dining car and tossed down martini's and joked with his lawyers, I went to a cozy, little salad bar and sipped smoothies and talked with my girl friend.

My girlfriend—not sexual, you dirty minded pervert—was Tina Garfield.

Tina was brunette to my blonde. Like me she liked to wear her hair long, with abundant tresses curling this way and that. She was into fitness, too, and she liked nothing better than looking good.

In fact, we liked nothing better than to look good. I tell ya, there is no higher feeling than strolling down the walk, heels clicking, feeling the male heads snapping around to take in our voluptuous curves, our outstanding mammary glands, our red, juicy lips.

But don't believe me, just follow me around some day and see for yourself. Giggle.

Anyway, we were sitting at a table in a corner talking girl stuff.

Girl stuff is a broad subject, no pun there, and it includes everything from the color of your lipstick to who's dating Shiela. Whoever Shiela happened to be at the moment.

And I told Tina all about the morning. And we giggled and laughed at how I had handled rough and tough Roscoe, and then we talked about her boyfriend, a hunk who worked as a lifeguard at—a shadow darkened our table.

"I'm sorry," a voice stuttered.

The woman was standing with her back to the sun and I lowered my sunglasses to better see her.

She was maybe 25, and a delightful, little thing. She had a darned good body, a pretty face, but her clothes weren't the best. Of course, I'm sort of a clothes snob, so...

I said: "Sorry for what?" My eyes got used to the sun and I saw that she was holding a bundle.

Across from me Tina was watched with a tilted head, her eyes all quizzical and puzzled.

"I didn't know what to do."

A bundle like a bag, a bag full of groceries...

"I didn't know who else to turn to."

...not a bag...a baby.

"Marsha, I told you you couldn't come here when Mrs. Tannenbaum was here." It was Pierre, whose real name was Roger, or something. He was our waiter and he took care of us personally. Now he hovered, and tried to get in front of the woman with the baby.

A baby. I may be into fitness and beauty, but, like any woman, I am a sucker for a baby. Durn things fill their diapers and do their little baby barf thing...and I just love 'em.

"I didn't know what to do!" She was actually crying now. Big tears. The kind that don't just mess up the make up, but wash it entirely away.

"I'm sorry, but you can't disturb our customers and—"

"Pierre," I spoke sweetly, "Please shut."

Pierre opened his mouth, considered me, knew that he had overstepped, and back away.

"The plot thickens," murmured Tina.

"Sit down," I offered.

The woman, Pierre had called her Marsha, didn't sit. She just stood there and sobbed. Cried all over her baby.

Tina stood up and pushed a chair under Marsha. Now she was sitting, gasping and trying to control her tears. Might as well try to control Niagra Falls.

We sat for a long minute, then Tina offered, "Can I take the baby?"

Wordless, sniffling, Marsha handed the baby to Tina.

"What's his name? Or is it her?"

"Charley," sniffed Marsha. She had the look of somebody who has held a baby for a month straight, and now that somebody else was holding him she looked lost.

"Would you like something to eat?" I asked.

"No…I don't—"

I waved to Pierre, who was there instanter.

"Pierre, Marsha would like…?" I looked at Marsha.

Timidly, Marsha whispered. "Could I have a hamburger?"

Huh. Younger than 25.

"Yes, ma'am," he said. Now that the young lady was adopted by us she was a customer, and would receive all the respect that an upper crust establishment has to offer.

"Oh," I said. "That sounds delish. Can you change my order to a burger? Fries and a Coke, of course."

"Me, too," said Tina, cradling the baby and rocking him gently. She had one of those goofy smiles that women get when they fall in love with a baby.

Pierre nodded and whisked himself away.

"Now then," I said, shoving my untouched glass of water in front Marsha. "Please tell us everything."

And darned if Marsha didn't start crying all over again.

Marsha nibbled on French Fries. She had demolished that burger like it was the last burger on earth, or the first burger she had had in years.

"So I mismanaged everything. I thought I had the part sewn up, I was told I did, then the production company went broke, and then I found myself pregnant, and…"

She told us the tale of woe that is not all that common, but does happen, in Hollywood. Yes, young starlets come to town, but then they end up getting real jobs, or just return to Podunk, Nebraska to raise a family.

But this one hadn't gone home. This one had stayed and tried to make it, baby and all.

You had to admire her courage. Maybe not her smarts, but certainly her drive to make something better of herself.

"So you were slated for the lead in a series produced by…what was that production company again?"

"Starbright." She spoke like she had a secret and didn't want to say it. Of course.

"My husband had dealings with that production company," I said.

"Yes, I know."

And there it was. The dawn's light. The thought that bursts. The curse that ruins your life.

At that moment I knew it. And, female intuition, Tina knew it. And that was Marsha's secret.

So for a full 30 seconds nobody said anything.

Tina stopped rocking the baby, as he was asleep and making adorable, little baby sounds.

I stared, put my sunglasses back in place so I could stare from behind shields.

Marsha kept looking up, then looking down, nibbling a fry, looking up, looking down...

"I would like a paternity test."

Yet we all knew the results.

"I'm sorry, I don't—"

"Stop being sorry," interjected Tina.

"Yes, no more of this 'sorry' shit."

"But I don't know you, and I come here and..."

"And there was nowhere else to go."

"No. I have no family. I was an orphan, and—"

"So, here's what we're going to do." I spoke with the confidence of a woman who has made up her mind. Lord knows my confidence was shattered beyond all repair. "First, we're going to put you up in a swank hotel. No charge to you. And while you're getting room service and massages we will get the paternity test done. If everything works out, we will confront my husband."

"Confront...Roscoe Tan—" She couldn't even finish his name. He was a powerful figure, she was a failed starlet. What she hadn't grasped, yet, was that she had his bloodline.

"Yes. We will confront. We will make a plan. And if you really are in possession of Roscoe Tannenbaum's child, then you will never want again."

Marsha started crying again.

I said to Tina, "Hey, baby hog, give me the squirt."

Tina handed me the sleeping baby and I cradled him, and my heart felt warmer than toes over a fire.

Roscoe Tannenbaum's future looked up at me and smiled a toothless grin.

CHAPTER THREE

I had dreamed of a baby in my waking dream that morning. Intuition? Some weird sort of prescience? Probably. Being in California I get accused of being part of the loony tune, peace and love, save the planet cult, but that doesn't mean these things don't happen.

And, to be honest, while I don't spend my millions on gurus in spandex selling tea leaf theory, I do believe there are things of the human spirit that should be explored, and definitely not denied.

So, to explore the fact that my husband had a baby by another woman.

The baby was two months old. So Roscoe had boffed little Miss Marsha some 11 months previous. We had been married 23 months. So he was a cheater, and a bastard, and a lot of other bad names.

What do you call it when a woman is cuckolded? I know. Cuckolding is when the wife steps out. But what do you call it when a man steps out?

As we drove away from the restaurant I glanced at the other ladies.

Tina was in the back seat, arms spread out and sitting like the Queen of the May. The top was down on my Maserati, and she did so love the way the wind whipped her hair in the wind.

Marsha sat in the front seat, rocking Charley and cooing to him, and nervous as a cat on a hot solar panel. Hell, the woman had been preyed upon, found herself on the streets, and had just had her first meal in what was likely ages.

And it was a miracle baby Charley hadn't suckled all the milk out of her skinny, little breasts. (Well, once they were big, and she still had the shape, but you know how gluttonous little babies can be, right? Suck the nipples right off the tit if it was left up to them.)

"Siri," I asked my dash mounted cell phone, "what is the female equivalent of a cuckold?"

Siri, stupid as always, asked if that was the correct address. I said no, and the bitch actually asked me if I wanted directions or to make a phone call.

Tina laughed outright, and even Marsha tittered.

"Well, do better, bitches," I commanded caustically.

Tina, of course, rose to the challenge. She opened her cell phone and googled, then told me the answer.

"It's a cuckquean. It's supposed to be a fetish."

"I've got your fetish right here," I groused.

"Sounds like it's more of an everybody knows kind of thing, the husband seems to control it, the wife has to ask permission to be involved, that sort of thing. So what are you going to do?"

"Huh," I grunted. Truth, I felt like driving my precious, little Maserati into a light pole and handing Roscoe the bill, and laughing in his face. There were several things stopping me, however.

First, the price of a Maserati isn't much to a tycoon like Roscoe. Pocket change, if you get my drift.

Second, it was my car, and I loved it, and what was the point in hurting myself? It was Roscoe that needed the hurting.

We pulled up to my doctor's office and we strolled into the veddy expensive clinic like we owned the place, which, if you consider how many friends I had sent there for plastic surgery, we did.

"Is the Doc in?" I asked the nurse at the front.

She smiled professionally, recognized me, and immediately picked up the phone and pressed a button. "Dr. Patterson? Mrs Tannenbaum is here. Uh, huh." Hung up and said, "He'll just be three minutes. Would you like coffee, tea, or…?" she arched her eyebrows in question.

"No, thanks. We'll just lurk a bit."

I led my two girls and brat over to the door leading to the back area. I nodded for Marsha to sit. Tina folded her arms and leaned against the wall facing me. I folded my arms and leaned against the wall.

Behind us, at the counter, the nurse kept glancing us. Our behavior was out of the norm, but she managed to contain her curiosity and pretend she was ignoring us.

"So, girlfriend. What's the haps?" asked Tina.

I smiled. It was the kind of smile that could freeze boiling lava in under second.

"Anything exciting been happening lately?"

I lowered an eyebrow and frosted her again.

She laughed. "Would you like to purchase a gun? Fully automatic? Guaranteed for 50,000 rounds?"

"Now you're talking," I muttered.

She grew sober. "Seriously, what are your plans for dealing with this little imbroglio?"

"You mean beyond an enema with a ten foot railroad spike?"

Tina grew silent and watched me. I had started talking, all she had to do was give me the silence and I would be forthcoming.

I sighed. "So I find out my loving hubbie has been making babies without my permission. What should I do?"

Tina shrugged. She waited. She was a wise girl.

Sighing again, trying to calm myself down, I said, "At first, all I wanted to do was make him suffer. But how do you make a guy richer than God suffer? I could divorce him, but, I hate to say this, I love him."

I didn't say anything for a moment. Then: "If only I could make him feel the hurt I feel. How it feels to be betrayed. How it feels like to be a woman..." I stopped. Little lights going off in the back of my mind. Little avalanches sliding around inside my head. Thoughts ganging up on me and forcibly opening my mind.

"What?"

"If only," I started again. "If only I could make him understand what it is to be a woman, and to..." My mind sort of short circuited at that moment. I had said it. I had pronounced sentence on the cheating bastard. I just had to figure it out. My half statement, if taken as whole, to make him feel, to understand, what it was like to be a woman...then...then....

Then the door opened and Doctor Patterson smiled out. "Mrs. Tannenbaum! How wonderful to see you! Come in!"

Quickly we trailed after him to his office. Me, then Tina, then Marsha and the swaddling babe.

His office was stylish, done in green clothe with nary a sign of a medical instrument. This was where the close was done. This was where he sold the tricks of his trade. Very professional.

He made sure we were comfortably seated, then sat down himself. He sat down behind an acre of polished hardwood. Not a pencil nor basket upon the thing. Just a sheen that reflected faces accurately.

"What can I do for you today?"

"This is Marsha Carson. I would like you to do a paternity test on her."

A blank shield dropped around the doctor, and I knew what had happened. I was the client, but my husband paid the bills, and he and my husband, dear old Roscoe, were part of the 'old boys' club.

But I, of course, was a member of a bigger club. I was part of the females of the world, biggest damn club in the world, and I had a cause.

Heck, I had a mission, and possibly a jihad. And he, wise, old doctor, could read that in my oh so beautiful face.

He regarded me, framed his words, sighed, framed more words, then simply gave up.

"And the presumed father?"

"Roscoe." I said it flatly.

He sighed yet again, then he tried. "There are laws concerning the revealing of medical information…"

I slid in, as if with a knife. I leaned forward slightly and, as coldly as I could: "I need the results today. I don't need a copy. This can all be off the books. Nobody need ever know that you even gave the test."

I watched his throat work very slowly. It was a gulp. A slow motion gulp that revealed that he didn't like being the subject of my broadsides.

"Yes, but—"

"Furthermore, while you are quick walking the test to a conclusion, I will be going to the bank and taking out $5,000 cash. I presume that will be enough for this service?"

"It…I don't…you must understand…" he faded away. He gave his final sigh.

I waited.

Slowly, as if by pixels, he seemed to relax. He had come to a conclusion regarding my dastardly request. He looked at Marsha, "If I can have a look at this little charmer."

And, as the good doctor bounced Charley on his knee, a nurse was called to begin the test, and it was the beginning of the end for Roscoe Tannenbaum.

That afternoon we sat around the pool and sipped Margaritas. Real Margaritas made by Jaunita.

Well, Tina and I drank. Marsha sipped a Coke. She worried about the effect of alcohol on her baby milk. It was obvious that she was a good mother. Yes, she had fallen on hard times, and her story indicated that she hadn't been the sharpest Ginsu in the drawer, but she had a good heart and was trying.

"So, what you going to do?"

"I want to change him into a woman."

Tina spit out half a gulp of good Margarita. "You what?"

"I want him to know what it feels like to be a woman."

"Roscoe T? The Man himself?"

"Maybe it's time 'The Man' learned what is like to be 'The Woman.'"

"Jesus. You're serious."

"As serious as a castration."

Tina gave a mock shiver. "Please don't say that word. I like my men to have all their parts."

At that moment Juanita came out with another tray of Margaritas. She placed them on the wrought iron table we were sitting around and started to leave, but I said, "Juanita, could you please have a seat?"

Tina blinked. I could see she was having trouble with my bringing the servants into this.

Hesitantly, Juanita sat down. I pushed one of the Margaritas towards her. "Drink, girl, we have some serious business to discuss."

Juanita gripped the glass, her hand tight around the stem, and lifted it to her mouth. She looked at me for a moment, and then, perhaps because she needed to imbibe a little to enable herself to deal with things out of the ordinary, she took a big gulp.

"I'm going to change my husband into a woman," I said. "And there are going to be times when I will need your help."

Juanita's dark, Mexican eyes grew round and liquid. "Muxe?" she blurted.

"If you mean a man who becomes a woman, then, yes."

The woman had a fit, without moving, right in front of me. I half expected her to make the sign of the cross and running screaming from my home.

But I should have known better. This was an old Mexican lady who had seen good times and hard, who had raised children, and put up with the peccadillos and felonies of the opposite sex.

Juanita, who had helped me drag my drunken husband to bed, was built of stern stuff. After the gulping and wide eyes and the heavy breathing and looking around as if to see who was listening, she giggled. Actually giggled.

Tina laughed.

Marsha smiled wanly. She was a good girl, and she didn't know how mean and vicious high class people like myself could be.

"What do I need to do?"

So we began talking about clothes and make up, methods for forcing the transition, how to deal with Roscoe's temper tantrums, and other bits and pieces of the coming production.

And the pool man showed up. A studly, Greek God sort of fellow, a little middle-aged, but still rippling with muscles, a surfer's haircut, and the look in his eyes that told us he was a struggling actor.

Of course. Everybody in Southern California wants to be an actor. Why would he be different?

"Hey! What's your name?" I called out.

He stood there, festooned with long poles and hoses, and said, "Dick."

"Oooh, I like that name," bubbled Tina.

"Well, Dick, come over here and have a Margarita. I need your advice on matters of world importance."

Dick came and sat down next to Tina. Well, actually, he sat down on the chair next to Tina, and then my girlfriend sort of crawled into his lap and started licking his face.

Now, truth be told, we were getting sloshed. Juanita had kept up the flow of world class Margaritas, our favorite liquor store, the Pink Dot, was keeping us supplied with endless bottles, and I was starting to slur my words.

Well, truth be known, I needed this. Not only had I been betrayed, but I hadn't partied like this for years. Maybe a decade. I had been too preoccupied with how I looked to have a truly good time. So I was having a good time.

Tina: "Hi, DICK! I love your name. DICK. Do you think you could do your name to me?"

And Dick said the funniest thing I had ever heard. "Actually, I'm gay."

We all laughed hysterically. And Tina cursed. Then Tina said: "I'm going to convert you." And we all ooohed and awwwed and pitied the DICK.

"So what is this problem you need my advice on?"

In his defense, he wasn't drunk, and so was still serious.

"My husband cheated on me so I want to make him into a girl."

"Cool," he nodded thoughtfully, not put off a blink, even though he was sober, by my outlandish statement. "Where do we start?"

And so the afternoon went. More and more people showed up. More and more bottles showed up. More and more Margaritas disappeared. by the time Roscoe arrived home, fashionably late, I might add, there were 40 or 50 people in the house and overflowing the pool area. The sound system was working at full pitch and The Doors were telling everybody it was 'The End.' Neighbors came to complain about the noise and were absorbed by the frivolity and festivity. Cops came to issue citations, so we called the mayor who called the police chief who called...and the cops disappeared. Or went off duty and joined the party.

And, I might interject, Marsha and Charley had been whisked away to the Beverly Hills Hotel, where they were enjoying a sedate and sober, and relieved, night.

Anyway, to get back to the story, all the people who were at the party, close friends or passersby, were asked their advice, and help, on the production dealing with turning Roscoe Tannenbaum into a woman.

And they all had sage wisdom and good ideas to add to the mix. And they all laughed and said it was a good idea. And...I want to make a point here.

Some of you dear readers may be wondering how I expected to be able to pull off this absolutely stupendous practical joke. And it was becoming known as a great joke. Heck, even though I talked about Roscoe as a cheater, and even seemed a bit vindictive, everybody automatically classified it as just one more practical joke.

To be truthful, they probably had to. To consider my plan as nothing but the projection of a jilted female would have resulted in people walking away, and nobody wanted to walk away. So it was classified as, accepted as, a practical joke.

And why didn't they want to walk away? Because they had all, close friends and passsersby alike, been the victim of my husband's practical jokes.

The mail man had reached into the mail box and put his hand in a pile of dog doo.

Our neighbors woke up to find their lawn painted purple.

DICK had been cleaning our pool, and found out that his cleaner had been replaced with soap, very sudsy soap.

Everybody...EVERYBODY...had felt the bite of my overzealous husband's sick and twisted sense of humor.

So they were all willing.

And here is the crux...if I had asked everybody to keep a secret, everybody would have told. They would have giggled and blurted, and called the local news, and written emails and twitters and committed every other sort of communication to the world at large. Roscoe would have found out about my plans long before he ever arrived home.

But in telling people that it was all just a practical joke, NOBODY said a word. Nobody could have dragged the truth out of them, not even with Budweiser horses.

EVERYBODY wanted to be part of the grandest practical joke of all time...EVERYBODY wanted a little revenge for the constant trickery Roscoe had subjected them to.

And, by the time most of them sobered up, most of them had forgotten the conversations. They just figured it was drunk talk and life went on and that was that.

Heh. Heh.

This has been the first three chapters from

I Changed My Husband into a Woman!

Read it on kindle or paperback

Printed in Great Britain
by Amazon